Chockie

Printed in the United States of America

First printing June 2020

Kenneth R. Luchterhand
ISBN: 9780578686196 paperback
ISBN: 9780578688473 hardcover
ISBN: 9780578688466 ebook
BISAC: Fiction/ Middle School/Pets/Bullying/Mystery

Chockie

~

KEN LUCHTERHAND

Also by Ken Luchterhand:

Kema's Journey

Dedication

This book is dedicated to my son, Kennan. He has been a positive influence in my life and the lives of everyone who knows him. His happy, energetic attitude is contagious and makes my days much brighter. I know he has a bright future ahead of him.

CHAPTER 1
The Pet Shop

I DON'T KNOW WHAT I was thinking. I agreed to go along with my mother to town. She wanted to do some shopping and she asked me to go along with her.

I hate shopping. I guess I agreed just to make her happy. A kid has to do that once in a while.

"Peter, be back to the car by 3 o'clock," my mother told me from beside her parked car as she handed me a $5 bill. "I only have a few things to pick up before your father gets home."

"Okay. See you then," I said. I looked at my wristwatch to figure out how much time I'd have to waste. I didn't want to follow my mother around while she shopped. That was boring. Instead, I just wanted to look around in the small shops along Douglas Creek's Main Street, which was only three blocks long. I could stand anywhere along Main Street and see both ends.

I walked down the cracked and uneven sidewalks,

looking into each of the store windows as I passed. I remembered many more stores being open, but now "For Rent" signs were propped up against the insides of the windows.

Holding the wadded up money in my left hand, I set my sights on the root beer stand on the corner across from the bank. An ice cream cone or a root beer float seemed about right on such an unusually hot day.

Walking at a swift pace, I suddenly froze in my tracks. Some boys were walking toward me on the same sidewalk.

One of them was Ralph Higgins.

I gazed around for a way to avoid him. To my left was a store door, so I quickly pulled it open. Bells rang from above the door and quickly, I darted in.

What I didn't see and didn't expect was someone on the other side of the door who was about to exit.

The woman shrieked as I ran into her, knocking the brown paper bag she was carrying onto the floor. The woman backed up with a shocked look, then looked down.

I noticed whatever was inside had burst and water gushed out onto the floor. The bottom of the brown paper bag had split open. Along with the water running every direction on the floor was a small goldfish, flopping about.

In almost a panic state, I swiftly stuffed the $5 bill in my pocket and scooped up the fish in my hand. The fish was putting up a furious fit of slapping inside my cupped hand. There was no time to waste. I saw an aquarium near the counter, only a few feet away, and made a dash for it. Quickly lifting the plastic door at the top, I tilted and opened my hand, allowing the fish to drop into the water below.

"No!" a man yelled from behind the counter. "Not in that tank!"

I became alarmed as the young man, his sleeves rolled

up, walked fast toward the aquarium. My eyes went back to the fish inside the tank. I wondered what I had done wrong, turning my head to watch as the goldfish shimmered in the water, light flashing off its scales, as it descended and began to swim back to the top.

I was in such a hurry to save the fish that I paid no attention to what was in the tank. One of the two fish, large and dark with a complex of red markings on its sides, dashed over to the goldfish and quickly snapped it up.

"Oh, no!" I exclaimed, frozen in time, staring in disbelief at what had just happened.

The man stopped a few feet away, realizing he was too late.

My shoulders slumped in resignation.

"Oh well," he said, looking at me and breaking into a smile. "It's just one less goldfish I have to feed to them later."

I looked at the man and back at the fish, my mouth hanging open. "What are those?" I asked, pointing at the aquatic critters I now considered monsters.

"Oscars. They love to eat other fish, especially goldfish."

The woman picked up the wet paper bag between her thumb and forefinger, the empty plastic bag in the other. She glared at the man and then at me.

Her silence spoke volumes. I looked at the man with dread and then dug my hand into my pocket to retrieve the $5 bill. I held it out to the woman.

She shook her head. She wouldn't take it.

"It's fine," the store clerk smiled and quickly responded before I could say anything. "Tell you what – why don't we pick out another goldfish. We have plenty," he said to the woman. He turned toward the room at the back of the store with rows of aquariums and she followed, glancing back to give me the look of shame.

I felt like I had done something horrible.

I stood out in the main area, where I could hear the man and the woman talking in the room with all the fish tanks. It sounded like the woman was being very particular about which fish she wanted while the man was being very patient and accommodating. Meanwhile, high-pitched squeals emanated from the tanks on shelves along the wall near me. Guinea pigs dashed about in a couple of the tanks, while hamsters, white mice, white rats, and gerbils occupied other tanks.

When her new goldfish had been bagged, the woman exited the back room and went directly toward me.

The store clerk was a few steps behind her.

"I want to apologize for being so angry, young man. I know you didn't do it on purpose," she said, holding out her hand limply for me to shake.

I grasped her hand reluctantly and shook it.

Dropping my hand, she cradled the brown paper bag in the crook of her arm and departed the store.

I glanced over to see the man watching the interaction.

"See there? No problem. Everything is okay," he said.

"Yeah, right," I said sullenly.

"Now don't be so down on yourself. You did every-thing right. You had no way of knowing those two fish were man-eaters," he said with a smirk, extending his hand toward the tank with the Oscars at the front counter. "My name is Mitch." He held his hand out to me. Mitch looked like he was in his mid-twenties, tall and slender with scruffy hair and like he hadn't shaved in three or four days.

"Peter," I said, shaking his hand. "Peter Brighton."

"Nice to meet you, Peter," Mitch said. "Brighton, huh? Say, your father wouldn't happen to be Jim Brighton?"

I paused for a moment, then turned to look into an aquarium. "Yeah, that's my dad."

Mitch seemed surprised at my reaction. He quickly changed the subject, "You ever been here before?"

"No."

"Tell you what. Let me give you a quick tour of the place."

I looked toward the fish room entrance.

Mitch followed my gaze. "Come on, I'll show you."

My eyes widened as I stepped into the room, which was dark except the lights emanating from the aquariums. The aquariums were arranged in two rows, one row at eye level, and one row at my knees. The room was arranged in a horseshoe shape, with two rows on the right side, two rows on the left side, and two rows in the back of the room. Also, there was a center island, with two rows of tanks on either side, with a counter on the end.

The whole atmosphere was rather surreal for me – like nothing I had ever experienced. It was like I had entered another world of some awesome underwater scenes I never knew existed. I stood right beside the fish, the coral, plants, and the bubbling treasure chests.

A bubbling sound came from everywhere, like something exciting was happening all around me. The soothing hum of a big air pump in the backroom provided a steady noise seeming to add to the vibrancy of the environment. The smell of the warm, moist air was heavenly.

Immediately immersed in the scenes and the fish, I glanced from aquarium to aquarium, realizing I was smiling.

The outside world melted away, as I became more and more absorbed in the underwater scenes.

Canary yellow, cobalt blue, and scarlet red fish hastened about to the front glass as I approached. They were dashing into cracks and crevices of a few rocks stacked at the bottom of the tank.

"These are African cichlids," Mitch said. "Have a look around. If you don't mind, I need to finish cleaning this tank, but I'll be right here if you have any questions." He removed water from one aquarium with a hose that extended into the back room, briefly returning to talk to me for a while and then returning to his task.

I watched for a time and then moved to the next tank, which was full of beautiful bright red, blue, green flat-sided fish, all in a circular shape about the size of a half-dollar coin. The name on the tank said the fish were 'discus,' going for $30 each.

Several tanks held goldfish, some just like the one the woman dropped outside, but I noticed a great difference in the various types. There were some with huge eyes, some with colorful orange, white, and black markings. Many with extremely elongated fins and still another kind with long, slender bodies called 'koi,' as was written on the side of the aquarium.

I moved on to the next tank with a multitude of colorful fish swimming in every direction around coral. At the bottom of the tank, some creatures had many tentacles that waved back and forth with the water movement. I noticed some type of bar at the back of the tank that produced a multitude of fine bubbles and a kind of hissing noise.

"These tanks are saltwater," Mitch said to me, pointing to a whole bank of aquariums along the mid-level shelves. "The fish live in the ocean."

I moved to another bank of aquariums with many kinds of smaller fish.

"These are the community fish, what we call our 'bread and butter' fish," Mitch said. "These are the ones we sell the most – the fish that get along together. Most people buy these because they can all go together without harming each other."

I took my time looking at all the fish in those tanks and then progressed around the center island to the other side. I kept looking at aquariums on both the other wall and the center island. Just ahead was the other opening to the fish room.

In the eight end tanks, there were some very large fish about a foot long. They began splashing their tails at the surface, noses planted to the front glass. They were interested in my presence, it seemed.

"Those are the Central and South American cichlids," Mitch explained. "They think you're going to feed them."

I thought of them like dogs, wagging their tails, looking at me, expecting a handout.

He went over to a shelf above the bagging counter, twisted the cover off a fish food canister, and retrieved a handful of orange-colored sticks, each about an inch long and the diameter of a piece of cooked spaghetti. He handed them to me. "Go ahead. You can feed them if you want."

I took them into my cupped hands.

Mitch lifted one of the hinged glass covers on the tank with four large silver torpedo-shaped fish that had many black markings on the end of each scale.

I dropped about six food sticks into the top of the water.

The fish mouths quickly snapped up the food sticks, even coming to a short distance out of the water. I was surprised and jumped a step backward, wondering if I would get bitten. "Neat!" I said. "I like those."

Mitch closed the top.

I stepped back to look at the huge fish, and then watched the big fish in the big aquariums. The fish seemed to be more aware of me and their eyes seemed to follow my movements. "They're really friendly," I said, impressed with the way they interacted with me.

"Yeah, many of them become part of the family, almost like dogs. I guess you could call them water dogs," Mitch said. "They live around 10 years, so people really get attached to them and usually give them names. The most popular are Oscars, like the ones you saw up in front of the store."

"Oh yeah," I said sullenly, remembering I fed that woman's goldfish to those two in the front of the store. The memory of this event made me sad. I gasped when I suddenly remembered my mother expecting me back at the car. I looked at my watch and felt stunned. "Oh my gosh! I was supposed to meet my mother 10 minutes ago."

"Well, you better get going then," Mitch said. "It was nice meeting you, Peter. Come back again."

"Bye," I said as I turned and rushed out the door.

Running down the sidewalk, I headed for my mother's car, parked about a block from the pet shop.

The car was in sight when I saw someone walking toward me – someone who made fear rise into my throat. It was Ralph again, the big kid who often teased and gave me a difficult time. I was hoping he didn't see me yet and I dashed for my mother's car before I met up with him. Through the rear window of the car, I could see my mother sitting in the driver's seat. I hoped I could get into the car before I met Ralph on the sidewalk. I could only imagine him running me down once he caught sight of me.

I didn't see the police officer at first. She was a young woman in uniform with a small black box in her hand, walking down the sidewalk next to the parking meters. She was checking each one for the amount of time left. Stopping at the meter at my mother's car, the policewoman looked at the front license plate and wrote something on her equipment, then went back to the parking meter.

"Wait!" my mother yelled as she exited the car and hurried to the front. She began to talk to the policewoman, which was just enough distraction to have Ralph stop for a few seconds to watch what was going on. This allowed me to get away from him. I ran up to my mother and stood close while my mother pleaded her case. I briefly looked over to Ralph before I diverted my eyes back to the policewoman.

I stood while my mother and the police lady talked, but I didn't hear what they said. My mind was elsewhere. My mother sharply took the ticket, walked around the car, and got in. I got in the passenger side, all in silence.

We rode home without either of us saying a word. After several minutes had passed, I took the ticket, made out to Laura Brighton, and saw that she had been fined $10 for expired parking.

Not a word was said until she broke the silence while pulling into the garage. "Thanks a lot, Peter," she said.

I could tell she was angry and holding back her words. "Sorry, Mom."

"What took you so long? Where were you?"

"At the pet shop. This woman dropped her goldfish and I helped her get it back ..." I swallowed before speaking again, "...into the water." I didn't want to explain anymore, the sight of the Oscar eating the goldfish replaying in my mind.

We were both quiet for an uncomfortable minute, which seemed like an eternity.

"That was very nice. I'm sure she appreciated your help."

"Yeah," I said.

I remained silent, not wanting to explain everything that happened. My mind went back to the sights in the fish room, where the underwater scenes and sounds took me away to another world. "Yeah," I said again, this time more confidently. I caught the sight of my mother glancing at me. I turned my head and stared out the side window, my mind going back to those colorful and interactive fish. I smiled.

"Good," she said, looking again to see the smile on my face.

CHAPTER 2
Field Trip

I RELUCTANTLY CLIMBED THE stairs of the school bus on Monday morning. I hated Mondays because it marked the end of the weekend. Weekends were nice relaxing times when I didn't have to worry about school. I was a little slow while climbing the stairs and the usual buzz of kids talking was very irritating.

When I made it to the top of the steps, I immediately began to look for an empty seat – preferably closer to the front. My arch-nemesis Ralph and his gang always sat at the back of the bus and I wanted to avoid him. By the time the bus arrived at my stop, most of the open spots were gone.

Eighth grade was tough enough without having to deal with bus bullies.

As I walked down the center aisle, I saw two places where I could sit, neither very favorable. One was directly in front of Ralph and the other was three rows further to the front. I took the one closer to the front.

Immediately, the harassment began.

"Did your mommy kiss you goodbye this morning, Petey boy?" Ralph shouted.

Other children burst out laughing and I felt my face on fire. I couldn't imagine how red it must have been. I turned my head and stared out the window, hoping they would stop.

"Hey, Petey boy, which hand did you use to wipe your butt this morning?" one of the three boys shouted.

I think it was Shawn, and the laughing began again. I often wondered if the other children laughed because they thought it was funny or because they wanted to please the bullies so they wouldn't get the same treatment.

No doubt, the bus driver heard the attacks but he never did anything to stop them. When the attacks first started a long time ago, I thought the driver would say something to put an end to it. However, when he did not, I lost all hope. I talked to the driver once about it, but Mr. Jacobs just said, "Kids will be kids. What are you going to do? There was teasing when I was a kid and there always will be."

I hated riding the bus, but I had to do it twice a day - once to school and once back home – with a lot of anxiety and fear. The only positive aspect was the bus ride only lasted 20 minutes. Sometimes the three boys lost interest after a while and talked about other things, so there were times it wasn't so bad. Still, it seemed the teasing occurred almost every day.

As the school bus pulled up to the curb at school, everyone grabbed his or her backpack and stood up to file out of the bus, cross the sidewalk, and enter the school.

Inside, I deposited my backpack in my locker and went straight to the junior high biology room, my first class of the day. I walked to the aquarium sitting on the far end of the counter in the back of the classroom. A sink was at the other end of the counter while below there were drawers for our projects and science equipment. Above the counter were cabinets with swinging doors, with various contents mostly only the teacher knew.

I'd looked at the aquarium before, but I had always been in a hurry to get to my seat before the second bell. So, I never gave it much attention. Now, with my newfound interest in fish, I wanted to take a closer look. The light on top of the aquarium was already on. I recognized some of the same fish I'd seen in the pet shop: brightly colored swordtails, guppies, a pair of black mollies and a sucker-fish called a Plecostomus. I decided my favorite fish in the tank were the silver angelfish, who came to the front of the glass when I came near. I guess they expected a handout of food, just like the fish I'd fed at the pet shop.

"Mrs. Richards, can I feed the fish?" I asked the teacher at the front of the classroom.

"Yes, go ahead," she said, dismissing me quickly, then turning her attention to teacher's pet Peggy Haskins, who was walking toward her.

I never really thought about feeding the fish before. I guess Mitch and my experience in the pet shop sparked an interest in the finny friends. Taking a pinch of flake food from the yellow and brown plastic container, I gently dropped the flakes onto the top of the water, causing the water to erupt from the tiny mouths snapping at the surface.

Crossing my arms on the countertop in front of the aquarium, I rested my chin on top of my arms and watched every move the fish made. My mind swam deep into the depths of the undersea world, over the bubbling treasure chest, through the ceramic archway, and among the wavering plastic neon green plants.

It wasn't long before Mrs. Richardson said something

loud and the students' chatter came to silence. Somehow, I must have blocked it out and I didn't hear anything she had said. I continued to watch the fish swim back and forth and eat the remaining food.

"Peter," Mrs. Richardson said, "could you please take your seat?"

As I turned around and took my seat, a few kids snickered. My face must have turned beet red.

A little blond-haired girl named Jeannie Brown, sitting three desks ahead of my desk, smiled at me.

I wasn't sure if it had to do with the humorous situation, or maybe, I was hoping, she liked me. I liked her. I thought she was the cutest girl in school. A few times, I caught her looking at me before. I didn't think I was anything special, especially compared to the big shot athletes like Joe Adamson and Dale Zombrowski. Everyone called Dale "Zoom" except the teachers.

"If you remember, today we'll be taking a field trip in conjunction with our recent biology lessons," Mrs. Richardson said to the class. "Now, I'm going to need all of you to take notes, because you're all going to have to write a report afterward."

Most of my classmates groaned.

I didn't groan because I felt excited about getting out of the school building for a while to enjoy some time outdoors. Yeah, taking notes was a pain, but I'd rather do that than sit at a desk all day.

Mrs. Richardson had always been nice to me. I think she could tell I had an interest in biology, especially in living creatures. She was really old, maybe in her 40s, but she was a nice woman. She had flaming red hair, which always caught me by surprise no matter how many times I saw it. I couldn't figure out how someone can have hair that color and still be human. She had a few wrinkles on her face, so I figured she must be close to retirement.

One thing I knew for sure, her favorite color was green. Even her eyes were green. Every day she wore a green-colored lab coat in class instead of the usual white. Everything else she owned was green, even the car she drove.

Mrs. Richardson announced that everyone should pair up and work together. Each pair had a checklist for the aquatic species they could find. The other biology class, normally held at a later hour, was to join us. They had been permitted to leave their class to go on the special outing.

I knew who I was going to team up with – my best friend, Tommy WhiteEagle. Tommy was a member of the Ho-Chunk tribe and I always loved to learn more about his family's customs and traditions. I especially loved to hear the stories about nature and animals that had been passed down through the generations. I also found it fascinating how his family was so close, doing everything together, and supporting each other. I never had that.

The other class arrived outside by the school bus and all of the kids climbed aboard. The bus took off for the DNR station about 15 miles out of town.

I noticed that Ralph was in the other class, so I made sure to sit with Tommy near the front of the bus. The ride was non-eventful, except for the ever-growing babble of the children and an occasional scream followed by a chastising from Mrs. Richardson.

The group unloaded from the bus and stood in the parking lot near the DNR station building.

Soon, an older man about Mrs. Richardson's age dressed in a brown uniform exited the building and stood in front of the children. "Good morning, boys and girls!"

The students answered with a loud, "Good morning!"

"Welcome to the Wisconsin Department of Natural Resources field station," the man said. "My name is Rick Johnson and I am a conservation warden. I'm going to help you with your assignment today. But first I'm going to tell you a little about our jobs in the great outdoors. What do you think Natural Resources employees do?"

Many hands flew into the air.

I knew the answer to that question, but I didn't like speaking in front of so many people, so I didn't raise my hand.

Mr. Johnson pointed to one of the girls at the front of the pack.

"They give tickets to people who don't have fishing and hunting licenses," she said. Many of the students laughed aloud. Her big smile quickly changed into a pout.

"Yes, we do give tickets for violations, but we do so much more than that," he said. "We are stewards of our natural environment, meaning we monitor the plants and animals and make sure they go on living in a healthy environment." Mr. Johnson then announced that we were going to investigate the aquatic life in a nearby pond. He gave us the rules, that nothing was to be destroyed and nothing we brought in was to be left behind.

Mrs. Richardson gave instructions about catching aquatic specimens, then we would be releasing them unharmed back into the pond. She handed out a long-handled net and a plastic pail to each team. "We're going to walk down this path to a pond. I want you to stick with your partners. When we get there, I want you to spread out, and working with your partners, fill your pails half-way with water. Then use your nets to catch whatever aquatic life you can find. When you catch something on your list, look at it closely and then mark it off your checklist. And I don't mean just fish. There are a lot of bugs and other smaller creatures living in the water."

We were told that we could spread out along the sandy shoreline surrounding most of the pond.

Mr. Johnson explained how the shoreline was shallow and tapered very slowly toward the middle.

"There will be no horseplay," Mrs. Richardson added. "If I see anyone splashing water or any other nonsense, you'll have to sit next to me on the shore the rest of the field trip, plus you'll have to write an essay. So, behave yourselves."

Mr. Johnson led the group down the trail with Mrs. Richardson at his side.

When the line of students broke from the cover of the overhanging trees, we saw the sun reflected upon the waters of the pond. A wooden sign on a post said 'Sunfish Pond.' The water looked deep blue but was crystal-clear from up close. The sandy beaches extended into the shallow waterline, with us students able to see small fish darting about in search of food.

Several students immediately took off their shoes and socks, ditching the pails and nets to wade into the water. Shouts of excitement immediately rang out, exclaiming how the water was warm and everyone should join them.

Tommy and I set out to capture the most different aquatic life from the rest of the students, so we walked down the shoreline a little further than the rest. Soon, we had our shoes and socks off, wading with our nets, peering into the water. As our feet sank into the sand, bubbles rose between our toes, giving us a tickling feeling.

Small fish would dart in and out of the shallows, even more so now, since we were disturbing the bottom. The fish would find small organisms to feed upon, but held their distance because of the possible danger from us.

Tommy suddenly saw a crayfish dart into some rocks as he walked along, so he quickly pulled the rocks apart, grabbed the crayfish with his thumb and forefinger on either side of the base of the tail. Tommy said he had caught crayfish before, so he knew how to pick them up without getting pinched.

"I got a crayfish," he yelled out to me, looking over in my direction.

I scooped my net skyward, out of the water with a *whoosh*. "I got some minnows!" I shouted as I held up my net, staring at the shiny fish flipping at the bottom, catching the sun's rays, and reflecting the bright light into my eyes.

Our attention was on the fish and other aquatic species, so we never saw someone sneaking up on us from behind.

I was bent over, looking at what I just caught when two hands suddenly pushed against my hip. The net flipped away from me and I crashed down into the water, my head completely submerged. I got back onto my feet as fast as I could; water streaming off my clothes and hair.

Tommy whirled around and started walking through the water toward Ralph.

Further back on the bank was Benny, a classmate who was not making any moves. By the look on his face, he was as shocked as Tommy and me, and he didn't want to become involved.

"What did you do that for?" Tommy yelled out in anger. It appeared that Tommy was about to give Ralph some of his own medicine.

I walked toward Ralph too, but a little more reluctantly than Tommy.

Tommy rushed forward and pushed Ralph in the chest, but it had little effect. Ralph swung his fists toward Tommy, landing one on the left side of his face.

I wanted to help him, but I didn't know what I could do since everything was in a flurry of motion.

"Stay out of this," Ralph yelled to Tommy. "This is between Brighton and me."

Tommy stepped forward, ready to land another blow. Both his fists swung fiercely and hit Ralph on the side of his head.

Ralph swung back, knocking Tommy's arms away.

A loud, angry voice could be heard down the shoreline.

"Stop! Boys, stop this instant!" It was Mrs. Richardson, yelling louder and looking angrier than I'd ever seen her. She was running up the beach.

The boys turned and froze at the sight of her coming toward them.

"I will not tolerate this type of behavior. Now will someone tell me what is going on here?" she demanded, breathing hard from her run. She got in the middle of Ralph, Tommy, and me, continually turning to briefly look at each of us in the eye.

None of the boys volunteered to say anything.

"I'm waiting!" she said.

After a few more minutes of silence, Tommy spoke up, "Ralph started it. We were minding our own business, collecting samples when Ralph snuck up on us and pushed Peter into the water. It was all his fault," Tommy said while breathing hard and pointing his index finger toward Ralph.

"Shut up, you big baby!" Ralph yelled at Tommy. "You're both a couple of big babies!"

"Is this true, Ralph?" Mrs. Richardson asked.

"I was just playing. They didn't have to hit me. They are the ones being mean. I did not punch anyone. They're the ones who hit me," Ralph repeated. He turned his head and spit into the water behind him.

"That was no play, Ralph! You tried to hurt me!" I shouted.

"That's enough!" Mrs. Richardson yelled. "We are going back to the ranger station and I don't want any more trouble. Not another word out of anyone!"

We walked single file back to the ranger station like prisoners of war. The DNR staff found separate rooms for us to sit in until it was time to go back to school.

Mrs. Richardson went back to the students at the pond.

It seemed like forever before she and the other students returned. On the bus ride back to school, Tommy and I had to sit in one of the front seats while Mrs. Richardson and Ralph sat across the aisle in the other front seat. Although the other kids were having a good time, none of us said a word on the way back.

When we got back to Mrs. Richardson's classroom, she told us she intended to write up a report on what happened today and give it to the principal. We were told we probably would be hearing from the principal at some point, but for now, we needed to go to our other scheduled classes.

The afternoon classes seemed to drag on, and when 3:30 came, I felt anxious to get home. However, when the bus ride started, I knew it would be a long, miserable ride.

I was sitting about halfway back on the bus when a baseball glove hit me on the back of my head. I immediately grabbed my head with my right hand, but I could already hear the laughter from several boys in the back of the bus.

"Hey Petey, what's the matter – can't you catch?" Mark shouted while chuckling it up with Ralph at his side.

"No wonder you suck at sports, Petey. Maybe you should

try out to be a cheerleader," Ralph exclaimed to the laughter of the other three boys. "Did you wear your dress today, Petey?"

I lowered my head and tried to remain calm, although I could feel my face burning with embarrassment. In the past, I tried firing words back at them, but I soon learned it only encouraged them to say more hateful things. My best line of defense was to ignore them and hope they went away.

Ralph kept talking to Shawn and one of them was rummaging through one of their backpacks.

I tried to ignore them and kept looking ahead. Maybe they would just forget about me and leave me alone.

As soon as a kid in the seat behind me got off the bus, Shawn walked down the aisle and sat in the seat.

Shawn moved his hands swiftly over the top of my head, placing something across my face and pulled it tightly.

"Auuwg!" I yelled, swinging my fist behind me while attempting to stand up and turn around in the same motion. I recognized the thing as an athletic supporter. My clenched hands were flying, hitting Shawn on either side of his head and occasionally in the face.

Shawn dropped the thing in the process and covered his head with his arms.

I felt disgusted when I thought about a jockstrap held against my face, especially on my mouth. It made me sick to think about it.

All the children on the bus watched as I unleashed my fury on Shawn, punching him with my fists, all the while tears coursing down my face.

"Peter!" Mr. Jacobs yelled, his eyes locked on me in the mirror over his head. The bus pulled over to the shoulder of the road. "Peter, get up here in front!"

I attempted to recover from the incident and walked down the aisle to the front of the bus, trying to keep from crying.

Mr. Jacobs had one of the younger children move from the front seat and made me sit in there. I didn't feel like explaining anything, so I sat in silence for the remainder of the ride home.

When I got off the bus, I went straight to my room, locked the door, jumped onto the bed, and sunk my head into my pillow. I stayed there, hoping the rest of the world would go away, even though the events of the day still swirled in my mind. A jolt ran through me when I heard a knock on the door.

"Peter, are you in there?" my mother's voice came through the door.

"Yeah Mom," I answered rather bluntly, trying not to let my strained voice give me away.

"Is everything okay?" she asked.

"Yeah Mom," I repeated.

"Well, it's suppertime, so please come and eat," she said.

I heard her footsteps trailing away and returning to the kitchen. I could smell the fumes of the hot stew wafting under the door and filling my room with the tantalizing scent. No matter how upset I felt, I couldn't deny my hunger.

I hesitated, not wanting to face anyone at the moment, but my stomach overruled any decision not to eat. I skipped lunch at school because I wanted to avoid eating in the cafeteria. When I walked into the kitchen, I saw the table had already been set. Mom usually asks me to do it. I felt uneasy about sitting at the table and possibly having to answer my father's questions, attempting to pry into the details out of my day. My mind raced, wondering what I could say to evade having any part of my torment blurted out at the table. Suddenly, my answer came to me. "Would it be okay for me to eat my supper in my bedroom?" I asked. "I have a lot of homework to do on my computer."

"What's going on?" my father asked as he walked into the kitchen from the living room.

"Peter has a lot of homework, so he was wondering if he could eat in his room," my mother answered for me. She'd always been that way, I'd noticed, often advocating for me. I knew I relied on her to protect me from any disagreements with my father, but I also worried about what strained relations I caused for my parents.

"Go ahead," she said to me. "I'll bring it to you." She shooed me along with her hand, indicating I should get to my room to avoid any more confrontations.

"Why do you let him do that?" my father asked. "You know we should all sit at the table for a meal. That is what the table is for. When I was growing up, the whole family had to be at the table. You let him do whatever he wants! You spoil that kid."

I heard the argument going on and I wanted to shut it out of my mind, so I closed the door and covered my head with my pillow.

A short time later, my mom knocked on the door and came in with a plate full of food. "So, what is going on?" she asked.

"What do you mean?" I said.

"Well, for one thing, you're not doing your homework like you said you were going to do," she said. "And another thing – I know you. I know when something is wrong. You're not acting like yourself. Peter … what's wrong?"

"Nothing. I'm okay," I said sheepishly, staring at the floor, trying to avoid her eyes.

"I know you better than that," she said. "You're usually engrossed in some Xbox games by this time and you're acting differently like you're sad or something. I am your mother…remember? Mothers know when something is wrong." She paused, fingers intertwined while held against her midsection. "So, tell me – what is going on?"

I looked at her, then back to the floor. "I just hate riding the bus," I said. After a long pause, I sighed and started again. "There are these guys on the bus." I tried not to get emotional as I went on. "They're giving me a hard time."

"I see," she said. After thinking for a while, she said, "Didn't the bus driver see it? Why didn't he do anything about it?"

"No. There is no real supervision on the bus. The driver never does anything to those guys. People can get away with murder," I said.

"Who is it? Who has been picking on you?"

"Ralph Higgins. Mostly Ralph."

"Well, we'll see about that. Meanwhile, I'll drive you to school tomorrow. Now eat your supper." She left the room, closing the door behind her. I could see that she was upset.

I just felt too ashamed to tell my mother everything that had been happening.

I felt all alone.

CHAPTER 3
Back to the Pet Shop

~~~

THE NEXT MORNING, I got ready like usual, but this time my mother drove me to school. She parked the car in the parking lot and walked into the school office while I went to my locker, then to my first class for the day. I was hoping no one saw me coming into school with my mother. Kids can be cruel and I didn't need any more teasing.

I didn't know what my mother accomplished, but I was distracted the entire time I sat in the classroom. I kept wondering what they were saying and hoping the rest of the kids wouldn't find out. I didn't listen to the teacher and I couldn't read because my thoughts were too jumbled.

The first chance I got that afternoon, I sneaked out the side door, cut through some trees, and walked down the sidewalk toward town.

Schoolwork wasn't holding my attention and there were other places I'd rather be, I figured. So, I ventured out and walked down Main Street with the pet shop in mind.

I've seen many of the stores close up and wondered if all the businesses would leave eventually. Many people would drive a distance to a larger city to do their shopping where the big stores offered everything cheaper and had a bigger selection. The local shops would suffer because of it.

From what my parents told me, Douglas Creek, Wisconsin, was once a bustling city, with a full variety of shops to serve the residents. The area had been founded on agriculture, in particular dairy farming. There were still a few farm kids in school, but when my mom and dad went to school, a majority of the kids in school lived on dairy farms, they told me.

My father grew up on a dairy farm. He said he and other students were allowed time off of school in the spring for planting and then in the fall for harvesting the crops. Farming had been the central focus of everything in the area.

Douglas Creek was named after the creek that runs through it, which is named after the founder of the community, Franklin Douglas. I think he was the first mayor or something like that. A dam was built a long time ago along Douglas Creek to form Mill Pond, which is a hub of recreation activity all year round.

Because the town had so few people, everyone knew each other. I think my mom and dad knew every single person in Douglas Creek. Of course, it helped that they were born here and had never moved away.

Since I found the pet shop in town, I thought maybe I'd go there to spend some time. I loved all the hamsters, gerbils, guinea pigs, ferrets, and birds, but my beloved place was the fish room. I remember how I felt like I could disappear into the surrounding darkness of the room, with the only illumination coming from within the aquariums. When I looked into the tanks, I could feel myself within the water, being right there with the fish. It felt like my private escape from the outside world.

When I entered the shop, Mitch was cleaning one of the aquariums used to keep some of the small animals but stopped what he was doing when he saw me enter the store.

"Hey, Peter, Good to see you again," Mitch said, brushing his hands on his pants. "No school today?"

Suddenly I got a little nervous, shuffling my feet. I hadn't expected to be asked that question. After running a few lies through my head, trying to figure out which one would be the most believable, I felt I was running out of time to give him an answer. The silence was unnerving. I decided to tell the truth, "Yeah, I went to school today. I just couldn't concentrate. Too many things on my mind."

Mitch stared at me, saw the expression on my face and I think he could see I didn't want to talk about it. I didn't need a lecture right then. "There's going to be a new shipment of fish arriving in about a half-hour. You can help me unpack the boxes if you want." He stopped for a moment and put his forefinger to his lips. "That is if you plan to be around. I don't want to hold you up if you have other things to do."

"No," I replied instantly, maybe too instantly. "I have nothing else to do."

"Okay, well, just hang out and I'll go back to cleaning the hamster and guinea pig tanks. The delivery truck should be here in a little while," Mitch said.

The store customer traffic was slow as the shop had just opened and most of the people came later in the afternoon or the evening, Mitch told me. Mornings were the best time for staff to clean small animal tanks, fish tanks, and birdcages.

I peered into each of the aquariums, taking more time to examine each species of fish and connecting them with the names written on the glass with a yellow wax pen. Even though I had seen them once before, it was all new to me then. Now I wanted to examine them closer.

I first looked at the commonly-sold community fish, such as guppies, platies, swordtails, glassfish, and tetras. Further down the line, I came upon cichlids, according to what was written on the glass. Some had the word 'aggressive' beneath the word 'cichlids.' The angelfish looked harmless, lined up at the front of the glass and staring at me. The African cichlids looked pretty, with all the bright blues and yellows. Next, were some firemouths, convicts, salvini, and severums.

I was staring into the next tank, one filled with some Oscars, a few called blackbelts, and some named chocolate cichlids, as indicated by the name on the outside of the tanks. For some reason, the chocolates caught my attention.

They were swimming back and forth, taking an occasional nip at each other. One chocolate ignored the rest of the fish, staying stationary at the front of the glass and looking at me. Occasionally, his tail would dip down and the fish would stand vertically in the water, then he'd bring his tail up so his body would come back up to a horizontal position. However, he never left his spot at the front of the glass.

The fish wasn't an ugly brown like the name implies, like chocolate candy, I observed. Instead, their heads and fins were more reddish than brown. Their sides were brown, but with a black line running down the middle of its side. Also, a huge black dot was positioned in the middle of its side and a smaller one at the base of its tail.

I looked closely at him, putting my face just a few inches from the tank while looking into the fish's eyes.

The chocolate never backed away, staring at me without wavering.

"Hi, Chockie. Your name is Chockie," I said, I couldn't help but smile. "You are such a cutie."

I looked at the tank for several more minutes and then moved on to the others, eventually ending with the saltwater tanks on the end. The saltwater fish were diverse and colorful but the fish somehow lacked the character and individuality I had seen earlier.

Going back to the cichlid tanks, I was again drawn to the tank with the chocolate cichlids. All the fish were swimming about and I looked closely for the one chocolate I'd been watching earlier. From within the colorful plastic plants, swam a singular fish, straight toward me.

The fish followed my every movement, swimming from one end of the tank to the other as I moved.

I could hardly believe it. I had a fish as a friend. It seemed like he picked me.

"I like you, Chockie," I told him. I didn't know if the fish was a boy or girl, but he kind of had a boy's face.

After a while, I went out into the main sales floor of the pet shop to look at the prices of aquariums, stands, hoods, heaters, and filters.

"Are you interested in setting up a tank?" Mitch asked.

"Yeah, I'd like to," I answered, keeping my eyes on the new tanks on display. "I just don't think I can afford it, though. I'm still in school and I don't have a job, so I'm kind of limited."

"Tell you what," Mitch said. "I have several tanks at home and there are a couple I'm not using right now. I have a nice thirty-gallon tank I could sell you. I have a cover for it, too."

"Well, I don't know. How much were you thinking you needed for it?" I asked.

"I'll make you a deal for it -- how about 30 bucks?" Mitch said. "And there are plenty of used heaters and filters in the back room. They are well-used and I can let you have a heater and filter. I even have a used aquarium stand that has been collecting dust. It won't cost you anything."

"That sounds like a great deal," I said. "I need to see if I can get the money. I'll have to talk to my parents. I'm not even sure they'll let me have an aquarium. If you don't mind, I'll let you know tomorrow."

"Hey, no problem," Mitch said. "No rush."

A loud buzzing noise came from the back room, as both Peter and I turned our heads in the direction of the noise. It kind of sounded like a noise from a doorbell-type buzzer.

"That must be the fish shipment," Mitch said as he turned and took a fast pace through the fish room, then through another door to the back of the building.

Mitch had left the fish room door open, so I could see a man in a dark blue uniform shirt and matching baseball cap enter the room carrying two stacked cardboard boxes with 'Live Tropical Fish' printed on the side. Outside, a large box truck was parked, with a rumbling diesel engine spewing exhaust fumes into the backroom as well.

Mitch blocked the door open and helped the delivery man, both making several trips to the truck to retrieve the boxes, then neatly stacking them on the floor in the back room. When they'd finished, Mitch signed a paper and the man took off, having delivered 15 boxes of fish.

"Well," Mitch said, placing his hands on his hips while staring at the boxes. "Looks like we have some work to do."

I didn't know what to say or what to expect. I couldn't imagine how fish could be alive inside cardboard boxes.

Mitch took two boxes and carried them into the fish room, where he cut open the tops of the boxes and flipped open the flaps to reveal a Styrofoam box inside. Taking the lid off, I saw many clear plastic bags neatly and tightly arranged inside the box.

Mitch removed one of the bags and held it to eye level, allowing the light from the aquariums to shine through the other side. "Discus," he said. "Red beauties. I wouldn't mind having these. Take a look."

I walked closer to look inside the bag. There were about a dozen red flat-sided fish, each about the size of a half-dollar coin.

Mitch took them over to an empty tank, opened the glass cover, and floated the bag on the surface. He went back to the box, pulled out another bag, identified the fish as angelfish, and then floated the bag in an aquarium with two remaining angelfish residents. "You can do the same," he instructed me. "Just grab a bag of fish, find the right tank, and place the bag on the surface. This allows the temperature of the water in the bag to match the temperature in the tank. In about 20 minutes, we'll open the bag and allow a little water from the tank inside the bag. This acclimates the fish to the tank water, so it won't be such a shock when we release them."

Mitch and I went through the same procedure until all the bags were floating, then took the rubber bands off to open the bags and allowed some water to enter the bags. Mitch occasionally would have to go to the front of the store when a customer entered or to answer the telephone. I felt completely comfortable working by himself and the experience allowed me to study each type of fish in greater detail. There were some fish I couldn't match up to ones already in tanks, so I waited for Mitch to help.

When all the fish were released, we leaned back against the counter and looked at the fully stocked tanks.

"Good work, Peter," Mitch said. "You're a natural."

I couldn't help but smile. "Thank you, Mitch. I had fun."

CHAPTER 4
An Aquatic World of His Own

~⁀

I LEFT THE PET shop and walked toward home. It was too late to go back to school even if I had wanted, plus my mother wouldn't be home from work yet. She often had house cleaning jobs in the afternoon. It was safe there. Our house was only about a mile beyond the city limits sign, so the walk wasn't so bad.

We lived in a gray ranch-style house with a full basement and attached garage. The roof was deteriorating badly and the rest of the outside of the house was beginning to show its age. I often wondered why my father didn't keep the house in better shape and spend a little more time on it. He seemed to spend all his spare time in the garage. My father's pride was his '68 Mustang and seemed like he treated that car better than he treated his own family.

I got home safely and when my mother arrived home, and later my father, neither one suspected I had skipped most of the school day. When my mother asked me about the ride home on the bus, I thought about telling a lie, but then confessed that I had walked home. She wasn't angry, knowing how I feared any more confrontations. She told me she had been promised by the principal that he would have Ralph sit in the front seat of the bus from now on.

Somehow, that information wasn't overwhelmingly reassuring. There was still Shawn and Mark to deal with, who I considered Ralph's cronies.

As soon as I could, I went to my room and looked up chocolate cichlids on the internet. I found that the fish, scientifically named Hypselecara temporalis, is a native of the Amazon River in South America and can grow up to about 12 inches, more or less. They have various shades of brown and red on their bodies. They aren't very picky about what they eat, are omnivorous – but love live food. They have a habit of standing vertically in the water, which comes from their ability to hang out in dense vegetation and snap up bugs from the surface of the water.

Chocolate cichlids can live about 10 years or more, and often become very interactive with their owners, it said.

That last part intrigued and captivated me: "… often become very interactive with their owners."

"Wow," I said.

Later that evening, I asked my mother if I might be able to have an aquarium. I knew my mother was in a sympathetic mood at the time and she would be more agreeable to allow me to have one.

"I have $22," I explained. "All I would need is $8." I told her about Mitch and his offer at the pet shop. I told her he was giving me a good deal on the aquarium and he was giving me several pieces of equipment.

"What I'm worried more about is who is going take care of it, especially when you lose interest in it," she said. "You know aquariums are a lot of work. You have to change water and—"

"I will," I interrupted. "I'm not going to lose interest. I have always been interested in fish. That's not going to change. I just never thought about having any until now."

"Alright, but I want you to keep it clean. If you don't – it goes," she said, pointing her finger toward the door.

I knew she was trying to be tough and lay down the rules, but I knew she wasn't going to be strict with me.

The next day, I was excited to get to school to tell Tommy about the aquarium I was about to get from Mitch at the pet shop and the fish that had intrigued me.

I convinced Tommy to walk down to the pet shop during our lunch break and we were late getting back to classes. But when we were there, I was able to pay Mitch and he had agreed to drop it by my house after school. I asked if I could come along because I dreaded riding the bus, and I'd really rather talk to Mitch about fish.

He agreed to take me.

Mitch picked me up from the school grounds a few minutes after school let out for the day. His old brown Ford Taurus was well used, but he said it got him from point A to point B without too much trouble. He was happy just to have wheels. The pet shop didn't pay much, he said, but it was good enough until he could save up enough to go to a private art school in New York City.

When we got home, Mitch first carried the aquarium stand and then the aquarium into my bedroom. We found a place for it, put the stand in place, and the aquarium on top of it.

Mitch told me what I needed to do to get the aquarium and equipment assembled and ready for fish. "Now, make sure you wait three or four days after setting it up before you add any fish. So start slowly. Only get a couple of fish and wait a week or so before adding any more. You need to get the nitrogen cycle going; otherwise, you'll lose all your fish," he said.

He showed me how to put the filter together and how to adjust the heater. He even brought a bag of gravel and a few used plastic plants for decoration. "Have any idea what kind of fish you want to get?"

"Earlier, I was thinking of piranha because they are cool, but I think I changed my mind. Besides, I'd go broke buying live food for them all the time," I replied. "Yesterday, when I was in the store, I saw some cichlids that I thought I might like." There was one chocolate cichlid in particular I wanted. I was a little worried that chocolate cichlid might be gone by the time my tank was ready for fish.

"Good choice. They are one of my favorites," Mitch said. "Just make sure you get some fish that are compatible and don't get too many. They are usually very territorial, so make sure you have a lot of structure in the tank, like rocks and driftwood, to divide the territories."

Mitch knew his stuff, so I appreciated the advice. I thanked him and said I would be in the shop in a few days, hoping to get some fish. I was still thinking about that chocolate cichlid, but I didn't know whether I should say anything about it or not. It might sound rather silly.

We said goodbye and finally, when Mitch was opening the car door, I ran out to the driveway. "Just one more thing....there's a certain chocolate cichlid in the store that I like. Do you think you could hold him for me?"

"Sure," Mitch said. "You have picked out a particular one?"

"Yeah, yesterday, when I was there, he came to the front of the glass and was watching my every move."

"It's going to be pretty hard to figure out which one. They all pretty much look alike to me," Mitch said. "But – I tell you what – I won't sell any chocolates until you come down and tell me which one."

"Okay, I'll try to get there as soon as I can. Maybe tomorrow – on lunch – if I can make it."

Mitch agreed, got into his car, and slammed the door. The door sounded like it might fall off but he made it down the driveway then drove away in the direction of town.

I got to work right away. I washed the gravel and dumped it into the tank, filled the tank halfway with water, arranged the plastic plants, adding a few big rocks here and there, and then filled the tank to the top with water. When I got the power filter going, the motor hummed and the water gurgled out at the top. Adding the cover and the light completed the project.

The lighted underwater world made me happy. To me, it was one of the most beautiful things I'd ever seen. I laid on my bed most of the evening, looking into its depths. Even my mother said it was *neat*.

CHAPTER 5
The Cafeteria

O NE OF MY least favorite places to go at school was the cafeteria. After all, it was full of noisy kids from all grades and, if I didn't have someone I knew to sit by, it could be terrifying. I didn't like eating alone.

I was hoping to skip lunch and go to the pet shop and tell Mitch which chocolate cichlid I wanted, but it was raining all day. I was stuck inside.

I entered the cafeteria with the hopes of finding Tommy right away with an open seat next to him. The wide-open room gave no refuge from the masses of kids. I always felt like hiding, but that would be impossible. The only thing to do in line is to try to avoid the staring eyes of the other kids. I hoped I would find somewhere safe to sit, hopefully with Tommy or another one of my friends, which was never a guarantee. It was a daily worry for me.

I slid my tray along the stainless steel counter, picking up a plate of something resembling food, a carton of milk, and then looking for a seat and a friendly face.

"Hey, Peter!" a call came from across the lunchroom.

I looked toward the opposite wall and saw a hand up in the air. I recognized it as belonging to Tommy. Relief entered my body and a faint grin broke out on my face as I made my way through the maze of lunch tables.

I didn't see the foot extend out into my path. I guess I was too busy looking at Tommy and the seat beside him.

The next thing I knew, my leg hit something suddenly, and my body went face-first toward the floor. I let go of the tray to catch myself with my hands against the floor. It was almost in slow motion, with the food flying everywhere and the crashing sound of everything hitting the floor echoing in my head.

After everything happened, there was silence.

Dead silence.

I got to my feet with spaghetti sauce all over my face and applesauce all over my shirt. I could feel every eye in the lunchroom looking at me. What was once silence turned into laughter. The roar was so loud, my face burned with embarrassment. I scooped up as much as I could from the floor and onto my tray.

Tommy gazed at me with a look of helplessness and shrugged his shoulders.

All I could think of to do was to get out of there. I turned around, briefly looking at the kids at the table where I tripped. I saw Ralph sitting at the end, wearing the biggest smile anyone could have.

The laughter subsided as I walked quickly toward the window to deposit my tray, but the sounds were forever ringing in my ears and my mind.

I walked quickly down the hallway, heading for the restroom to clean up the food on my face, shirt, and pants then made for the nearest exit. I heard the clip-clop of shoes behind me, but my mind was on getting out of there, removing myself from the embarrassment.

I just grabbed the handle to the boys' restroom when the person with the clip-clop shoes shouted to me.

"Peter! What happened back there?" Mrs. Connors asked, putting on her concerned look as she walked closer.

I had never known Mrs. Connors to care about anyone before this. "Nothing." I glanced at her then avoided her eyes by turning my attention to the door. "I just tripped."

"What did you trip over?" she asked. I could feel her eyes penetrating.

"Nothing," I said sheepishly. "My own feet."

"I see," she said, taking a deep breath, eyes scanning the hallway. "Well, don't you want anything to eat? You can go back in line and get something."

"No. I'm okay."

She looked at me, waiting for more.

The silence became unbearable.

"I don't want to go back in there. Everyone was laughing at me," I said. "I'd rather not."

She thought for a moment and then offered a solution. "Tell you what. Get yourself cleaned up and then come and sit in my classroom. I'll go get a tray of food and bring it to you. You can eat in there and no one will know."

I reluctantly agreed then went into the boy's room and wiped the food off my shirt with hand soap and water. Using paper towels the best I could, I tried to dry my clothes, then walked to Mrs. Connors' classroom. I felt uncomfortable being in her classroom all alone. I felt out of place and worried that someone, other than Mrs. Connors, might come in the door, see me and wonder what I was doing there. I just wanted to be alone.

"Darn it," I said to himself as I took a seat, then put my face into my hands. Tears began to flow and I was sobbing when Mrs. Connors walked in the doorway carrying a tray with food and a carton of milk.

She set the tray down on the desk across from me. Her hand rested on the top of my head as she bent down to speak to me. "What's going on, Peter?" she asked, a frown chiseled on her face. "Can you tell me what happened? Somehow, I don't think you've told me everything."

I took a minute before answering; having to subside my sobs and wipe away my tears on my shirt sleeve, "No, I'm okay. I guess I was just embarrassed about falling," I said.

"So tell me how you fell. Somehow, I don't think you're quite that clumsy. I'm betting someone had something to do with it. Am I right?"

"Yeah, well, could be. Someone's foot caught mine. Probably my fault though. I wasn't looking where I was going."

"No, I don't think any of it was your fault, Peter." She stared at me and sighed in resignation. "Maybe you don't feel comfortable talking to me about it, but can I recommend for you to see the school counselor? Her name is Mrs. Price and she's a very nice woman. She's dealt with this kind of thing before." Mrs. Connors got up and straightened out the chair. "Well, think about it. I think she can help you, Peter. You're a good student and I don't think you need any distractions like this. Will you consider it?"

I took a few seconds before answering and did so reluctantly, "Yeah, I guess so."

"Good," Mrs. Connors said. "I'll leave you alone now. You can just leave the tray on the desk. I'll take care of it.

Just know that we all care about you." She turned and left the room.

I waited until I was sure she was gone, then threw my empty milk carton across the room, which hit the white-board on the front wall. "Yeah, right," I said cynically.

CHAPTER 6

The Counselor

⌒ͻ

Just as I sat down at my desk in English class the next morning, the loudspeaker sounded, "Peter Brighton please come to the office. Peter Brighton, please come to the office."

All the blood drained from my face. I had never been summoned to the office before. This was usually relegated to the naughty kids, the ones who were always in trouble. I've always avoided trouble, but now all the other kids in school heard my name being called. I had now joined the ranks of the outcasts.

Slowly rising from my desk, my mind was racing. Should I make a run for it? Should I hide in the bathroom? These ideas ran through my mind. I dreaded what might take place, so I walked as slowly as I could down the empty hallway. My legs felt like jelly.

Having no other options and no time to figure out how to avoid my fate, my hand rested on the office door handle, pausing for a few seconds before turning it and entering. I scanned the office for a hint of what might happen. I wasn't sure what they wanted me for and what I would face.

Rising from behind the office counter, Mrs. Price, the school counselor, looked at me and smiled.

I stood there frozen.

"Peter," she said pleasantly but firmly. "Would you please come with me to my office? I would like to talk to you about something." Mrs. Price walked around the end of the counter and held open a side door for me.

I followed her down an inner hallway lined with office doors.

She walked until she reached the third door on the left and entered. "Have a seat," she instructed, sliding behind her desk and sitting in a comfortable-looking black leather chair. She impulsively straightened her suit jacket and looked as if she were thinking about the words she was about to say. "Peter, I asked you here partly because Mrs. Connors told me about an incident in the cafeteria that happened yesterday. I think that is just part of a larger problem and I want to help you, Peter. You have been a great student and until now your grades have been excellent," she said, pausing long enough to make me wonder what was coming next.

I'd learned long ago that when people tell you something bad, they always start by saying something good about you first. After that, they start telling you the bad stuff beginning with the word '*but*.'

"But recently, your grades have been falling." She picked up a paper from her desk, turned it around, and pushed it toward me. "As you can see, you are failing in three of your subjects and barely getting by in the others. I also have heard from some of the staff about some problems with you and other students." She sat back in her chair, interlaced her fingers across her lap, and took a deep breath. "I called you here to figure out what is going on. I'm sorry to take you out of class, but we need to talk about a few things. I also got a report about an incident that happened over the lunch hour yesterday. Would you mind telling me what happened?"

"It was nothing. Just a misunderstanding," I replied as I avoided looking at Mrs. Price and instead looked at the photos hanging on her walls.

"As I understand it, that was more than just a little misunderstanding," she said. "From what I was told, someone could have been seriously hurt. If that would have happened, no doubt there would have been an investigation and whoever was involved could be expelled from school. Now, please tell me what happened."

"I tripped."

"On what?"

"Just my feet, I guess." I didn't feel like talking about it. I just wanted to get this over and out of her room.

"Now Peter, if we're going to get to the bottom of this, if I am going to help you, you need to be honest with me."

An uncomfortable silence permeated the room.

"Ralph. It was from Ralph Higgins. He's the one who tripped me." I didn't feel good about saying his name, fearful that he might retaliate after finding out I told on him.

"I'll talk to Ralph about this," she said dismissively.

This is exactly why I didn't want to say his name. "No, please don't"

"Why not?"

"Because he'll just take it out on me later."

"No, he won't. I'll make sure of that. Now, what can we do to get your grades in better shape? Is there some reason you're failing in almost all of your classes?" She looked down at a paper on her desk, obviously some type of report showing my current grades.

"I guess I could try a little harder," I offered, but I was trying to please her so this all would end.

"I believe you can, Peter. You just need to put a little more effort into it. She sat back in her chair, looking at me and waiting for a reply. After a few seconds of silence, she resumed, "I'll talk with Ralph and get this whole thing straightened out. Let me know if anything with him happens again. Okay. You can go back to class now. I'll check back with you in a few days to see how things are going."

I got up and headed toward the door.

Briefly, I stopped, glanced back at her, and then continued through the door.

CHAPTER 7
Peter Buys Chockie

~⁀

I MADE MY WAY to the pet shop during my lunch hour, hoping to make it quick so I didn't get into more trouble for being late for my next class. When I entered the fish room, I went straight to the tank with the chocolate cichlids. I scanned the fish, frantically looking for the fish I hoped would be mine.

Mitch came over to stand beside me peering into the tank as well.

I was getting a little frustrated, not being able to discern one from the other.

Then, from behind some decoration, arose a chocolate a little larger than the rest. He came straight forward to the glass, again looking right at me.

"That one! There he is!" I was excited and pointed to the chocolate now swimming before us.

"Looks like he's taken a liking to you," Mitch said. "I've

never seen chocolates do that before. Sure, they'll follow you in hopes of being fed, but this one seems fixated on you."

I wasn't sure if Mitch was just saying this to be kind, or if he really meant it. Anyway, he said he had a good idea which one I liked, so he made sure it wouldn't be sold by marking the front glass with a grease pen.

'Hold - largest chocolate,' it said on the glass. He said he'd tell the other workers at the pet shop, as well. Some employees worked evenings and on Mitch's days off.

I returned to school, but I found it difficult to concentrate on schoolwork for the rest of the day. During study time, Tommy and I shared a table in the library and tried to get our algebra assignments completed, but often we were distracted.

Tommy took out his smartphone and began to show me the pictures he took of bald eagles when he and his older brother walked down by the creek.

I often thought Tommy must be obsessed with eagles because he often talked about them and took notice whenever one was within sight. "You sure like eagles," I whispered. "Why do you like them so much?"

"In our culture, eagles are sacred," he said. "Eagles have a special connection with the Creator. You can put your prayers on an eagle and it will fly up high to take them to the Creator. Also, it's my name."

"Wow…That's cool. Do you know much about fish?" I asked.

"Well, I know they live in water," Tommy said, obviously making humor of my question.

"No, I mean how are they viewed in Ho-Chunk culture?"

"You're excited about your new aquarium, aren't you? Well, according to what we have been taught, if you can make them your friend, they will guard and protect you," Tommy said. "That is when you are near the water. Don't count on them helping you on the bus or at school."

I had often told my friend of my difficulties with Ralph and his followers on the bus, and Tommy said that he wanted to help me, but it was difficult since we rode different buses.

I waited three more days before going back to the pet shop. At the advice of Mitch, I got a few inexpensive guppies to put in my tank to start the nitrogen cycle. That way, when the initial bacteria bloom occurs, if I lost a fish or two, it wouldn't be such a great loss. When the bloom subsided and the nitrogen cycle was underway, I could get the fish I wanted with less danger of losing them.

About three days after the introduction of the guppies, the water became cloudy, but then cleared up in a couple more days. A week passed and none of the fish died, so I felt it was pretty safe to get the fish I wanted.

I went to the pet shop with a bag of guppies to return to the store. I could hardly contain my excitement. The chocolate cichlid had been waiting for me and he would finally be going home with me. As soon as I entered the store, I looked for Mitch, but instead, I was disappointed to see a heavyset middle-aged woman at the front counter. She was talking on her smartphone and didn't even glance up to see me entering the store. She kept talking so much and so fast, I wondered if she would ever stop talking.

I went straight to the tank containing the chocolates, trying to pick out my favorite fish.

After a few seconds, the largest fish again moved to the front glass and stared at me. It even looked like the fish was swimming with enthusiasm, moving side to side with his lips pressed against the glass.

"Hi, Chockie!" I exclaimed. "I'm here to take you home!"

The heavyset woman waddled over to where I was standing.

"Can I help you?" she said in an unfriendly manner as if I was taking her away from what she would rather be doing – which was talking on her phone.

"Yes, I came to get a fish, that chocolate cichlid," I said while placing my index finger on the tank right where my chocolate cichlid held firm. "And I'm bringing back these guppies." I held the plastic bag out to her and she took them rather abruptly.

"Sorry, but those are sold. See, it says so on the glass." She pointed to the writing on the glass.

I resented being talked to like I was an idiot. I wished Mitch were here to help me. I considered leaving and coming back when Mitch was in the store, but I felt so excited to finally get my fish. The suspense had been killing me. "No, you see, Mitch wrote that on the glass for me," I said. "That fish is reserved for me."

"Mitch told me not to sell any from that tank," she said, almost snorting arrogantly.

"No, just the largest chocolate. That's because he's mine." I pointed to the writing on the aquarium. "It says so on the glass."

Either she didn't believe me or she was someone who loved making people angry. I have known people like this – people who had a chip on their shoulders all the time.

"Are there any other fish that you want?" she said.

"No, I just want my chocolate cichlid," I said. I could feel my face burning and I was getting upset with this woman.

"I told you – I can't sell any from that tank. If you decide on any others, let me know," she said as she turned and headed away.

"Look, can you call Mitch? He knows all about it," I said while walking after her. "I want to take my fish home today."

The woman went back to her cell phone on the counter and put it up to her ear. "I'll have to call you back," she said. "I've got an upset customer right now." After hanging up, she picked up the store wall phone, looked at some scribbling on a piece of paper on the wall, and pushed numbers on the keypad. "Yeah, Mitch, this is Darcy. There's a young kid here that says a fish in one of the cichlid tanks is his," she said flatly, then listened for a short time. "Oh. I thought you said I shouldn't sell any fish from that tank." She listened some more, then looked at me.

"What is your name?" she asked.

"Peter."

"He said his name is Peter," she said into the phone.

I heard Mitch talking, but couldn't make out the words.

"Okay, thanks," Darcy said, hanging up the phone. She went past me and headed into the fish room without saying a word.

I followed.

Going to the counter in the fish room, she placed a plastic bag into a clear, hard plastic box with a lip on it. She walked over to the tank with the chocolates and hung the lip of the box on the edge of the tank. She used a cup to scoop out water and pour it into the plastic bag. "Now, which one did you want?" she asked with a net in her hand, turning to look at me. She placed the net into the water, spooking the fish so they darted behind rocks, driftwood, and plants. They were all gone from view.

"I-I don't know," I said. "They're all hiding now." I wished she would back away from the tank, but I didn't want to irritate the woman. She already seemed to be in a bad mood. It looked like this woman didn't have much experience around fish. Perhaps she was more of a small animal person, I thought. "Maybe we should just let them alone for a minute, and then they'll probably come out better so I can see," I said.

Darcy stepped back and watched the fish for about a minute. They weren't moving, so she put down her net on the counter. "You let me know when you see the one you want," she said, walking out of the fish room and back behind the front counter. She picked up her phone again.

Not long after she left, the fish began to swim about. The largest chocolate came out of hiding and returned to the front of the glass. I removed the plastic bag from the box and floated it in the water. Most of the other fish hid again, but not the one I had named Chockie. Somehow, I knew it was him. I tilted the bag so it lay horizontal and the opening to the bag was submerged in the water.

Much to my surprise, the chocolate swam right into the bag. I tilted the bag upright, twisted the bag shut on the top, and took it over to the back counter where I twisted a rubber band to secure the top.

I walked up to the counter where the woman stood, talking on her phone once again. I rested the bottom of the bag on the counter and stood silently, waiting for her to ring up the sale. Upon seeing the bag with the fish, she said, "just hold on" into her phone and put it face down on the counter. "You're not supposed to bag the fish. That's my job."

I decided not to answer that statement, realizing it wouldn't get me anywhere, but instead stood silently.

The woman pressed numbers into the cash register, then pointed to the bag. "You only want one fish?" she said.

"Yeah. For now," I said. I wasn't about to bother her to get more fish because it was obvious my presence was interfering with her important conversation on her phone.

Besides, I wanted to become more familiar with Chockie and study which fish would make good tank mates with him first.

"Eight forty-two," she said.

I paid the amount, having borrowed the money from my mother again.

The clerk slipped the plastic bag into a brown paper bag, deposited the sales receipt inside the bag, and then handed it to me. "Thank you," she said insincerely.

I didn't bother to reply and slipped out the door.

When I arrived home, I floated the bag in my aquarium and later dipped water from the aquarium into the bag to allow the fish to get used to my water. After dipping water periodically for a half-hour, I tilted the top of the bag downward into the aquarium water and let the chocolate cichlid swim free into the tank.

Chockie sank to the back and bottom of the tank, breathing rather heavily, but his eyes were moving about, taking in his new surroundings.

"Welcome home, Chockie," I said.

I spent the rest of the evening in my room, as much as I could anyway, so I could watch my new friend's every movement. Chockie moved about the aquarium, eyes moving in every direction while looking at all the gravel and structure within the tank. I observed how it wasn't just mindless swimming, but rather a purposeful movement and to me, it seemed obvious the fish was thinking as he moved around while observing things.

Starting that night, before I turned out the light to go to sleep, the last thing I would do is say aloud, "Good-night, Chockie."

CHAPTER 8
Peter Goes to the Powwow

~~~

OVER THE NEXT weeks, Chockie and I developed a close relationship where he would come to greet me whenever I came into the room and even take food from my fingers when I held it near the surface of the water.

Chockie was often hungry and I was only too happy to oblige. As a result, Chockie was increasing in size at an amazing rate. I often worried about Chockie being lonely and needing a tank mate, but Mitch assured me that my fish was all right, especially if he had the frequent interaction I was providing. Mitch believed that Chockie now had established himself as the dominant fish and that any newcomers to the tank would not be granted a welcome situation. I was okay with this. He could be my only fish.

One day, Tommy invited me to an upcoming powwow the following weekend. At first, I felt uncomfortable because I wasn't Ho-Chunk or even Native American, so I was not sure I would be accepted among them. But after some persuasion, I agreed. Tommy told me that anyone is welcome and encouraged to attend their activities.

Tommy had his regalia and danced at every powwow he could, often winning in his age category in the contest. His regalia looked quite ornate, with bells on the ends of his leather straps and feathers on his butt in the fan shape of a turkey tail.

I wondered if I needed to have some type of ceremonial dress to attend, but Tommy said I didn't, that I could come as I was, unless I planned to dance in the contest.

The next Saturday, I joined Tommy at his house and then I went with his family to the powwow grounds a few miles east of the city near an old Native American village called "The Settlement," an English name that was given to the area by white colonists.

We arrived at the powwow grounds to see the parking lot nearly full with people walking everywhere and the rhythmic beat of a drum reverberating through the air. Also, the smells of all the food being cooked and sold by vendors permeating the air, including a favorite of mine - frybread. Frybread is a clump of dough that people cook in oil. I saw it being made at many of the food stands.

As we walked toward the arena, the center of all the activity, the drumbeats grew louder and we could hear the singers accompanying the drum. Multiple flag poles circled the arena and I saw many plaques with a name on each. I figured each pole was dedicated to a certain person. I'm not quite certain why.

Tommy and his younger brother Levi were partially dressed in their regalia but needed to put on a few more items before they could dance. The arena was round-shaped with sloped concrete seating to the top and ramps down to the center grassed dance area. The stands were filled with spectators, some in dance regalia, most not. Overhead speakers amplified the singing and drumming from the center of the dance arena, but it wasn't necessary. I could hear it loudly without the speakers.

The men's and women's regalia were both colorful, but the men's seemed to have more bells and feathers. Some had feathers in their hair, feathers on their legs, and feathers on their butts.

I noticed there wasn't any uniformity to their dancing. Some danced around the arena upright with just a little stutter-step, yet others twirled and bowed, pounding their feet into the ground.

Most of the women danced upright in a slow fashion, just shuffling their feet a bit, while others twirled. Then still, others performed a dance called 'scrubbing' by moving their hands and arms up and down at their sides at a fast pace, Tommy told me.

I kept watching all the activity in the dance arena while seated in the front row. This was something I'd never seen before. It wasn't long before Tommy and Levi had their outfits on and were dancing around the circle in a clockwise manner.

After Tommy and Levi had completed the first dance, the drums stopped, but then started again for the next dance. Tommy went up to me and grabbed my right hand, attempting to pull me out into the arena.

I resisted. "No," I said. "I don't know how to do it. Besides, I don't have the right clothes for this."

"Don't worry," Tommy said. "You can dance just the way you are. It doesn't matter. And it doesn't matter how you move. Just walk around and move your feet."

I didn't feel comfortable about it, but I got out into the dance arena. I moved around the grass arena beside Tommy, all the while I tried not to think about anyone watching me. The more I danced, the more I was comfortable. Soon I was having fun.

Following a lengthy session of dancing, Tommy, Levi, and I met with the rest of Tommy's family and bought some Indian tacos, which were like regular tacos but on frybread instead of a shell or tortilla.

When the day was over I felt tired but I had to admit, it was fun. They dropped me off at my home on the way to their house.

When I walked into the house, I had to tell my mother the details of the entire day. I went into my bedroom to lie on my bed and tell Chockie about my day. By the time I was done, I was very tired and I could barely keep my eyes open. I think I was asleep before my head hit the pillow.

CHAPTER 9
Peter Finds Underwater Solace

~~

OVER THE NEXT months, Chockie grew bigger and bigger. I developed a close bond with my fish. I wanted the best conditions for him, which included the best food I could get.

Chockie was too big for fish flakes anymore, so I switched to a type of food called cichlid sticks, which were specially made for larger fish.

When it was feeding time, I would hold a stick of fish food between my thumb and forefinger just beneath the surface. Chockie would come to the top and gently take the food from me.

"Good boy, Chockie!" I would exclaim each time.

I enjoyed my time with Chockie, but I can't say the same with my time at school.

Riding the bus had become a little less frightening because Ralph was required to sit in the front seat and his friends were less bold by themselves. I felt certain Ralph had instructed Shawn and Mark to keep up the insults, but I don't think they were so willing to do it when Ralph wasn't around. I still had to pass Ralph as I headed down the aisle on the bus, but I was counting on Mr. Jacobs keeping an eye on him.

I also knew my reprieve was on borrowed time. Someday, Ralph might serve his time and return to his back seat to resume his relentless attacks, maybe even more so because revenge could be foremost on his mind.

I still preferred not riding the bus and I'd do anything to avoid it, so I often pleaded for rides from my mother. She understood my frustration and fear, but she wasn't always able to give me a ride. A lot of times, she had house cleaning jobs, and taking me to school was sometimes inconvenient.

Ralph and I did see each other in the hallway at school, but for the most part, I was able to avoid any contact if I saw him coming. That is, until one time my classmates and I descended to the locker room to change for gym class, only to discover that the previous class was a little late in leaving. They were just finishing their showers and most of them were sitting on the benches between the rows of lockers.

The locker room was always a sweaty, smelly place, filled with dirty clothes, steam from the showers, and wet towels. The floor was always wet from the constant flow of wet feet coming from the showers back to their lockers.

When I entered the locker room, nothing could have prepared me for what was about to happen. The kids from the previous class were drying off and getting dressed. An area on the bench was vacant where my locker was located, so I walked past the other boys, sat on the bench, and turned the dial to the combination on my padlock to open my locker.

"What the heck?" bellowed a rather large boy, holding a white towel while dripping water onto the floor.

It was from Ralph.

"What are you doing in my spot, Petey boy?" he said tauntingly.

The other boys moved aside as Ralph walked toward me, never taking his eyes off me.

I stood up as Ralph approached, afraid of what he might do next.

Ralph placed both hands on my chest, grabbed two handfuls of my shirt, and slammed me up against the lockers. "Get away from my locker, you piece of crap," Ralph yelled, and then released his grip.

I turned without saying a word and saw all the other boys were standing near the end of the bench, not saying a word, and not helping either. I think they all were scared of him, too.

As I started to leave, Ralph turned and began peeing on my left leg.

"Stop it!" I yelled, getting away from Ralph and the stream of urine. "I'm telling!" I yelled. I was shocked and just wanted to run away.

"What are you going to do, tell the teacher that I peed on you?" Ralph said, then laughed.

I felt intimidated by Ralph's size and humiliated at what had just happened. I walked out of the locker room as fast as possible, not looking back and not knowing what to do about my wet pant leg that smelled like pee.

I didn't know where to go or what to do. I was more embarrassed about the incident than anything. If it just had been between Ralph and me, it wouldn't have been so bad. All the boys in the locker room saw what happened and news of it would soon be all over the school.

I ran outside and found a place to be by myself in a stand

of pine trees behind the school building. I couldn't stop crying. All my sadness and emotions were coming out and it seemed like I just might never stop crying. My body began to shake uncontrollably.

I didn't know how I would get home. I didn't want to ride the bus home and besides, I wasn't going to wait around at school that long. I just wanted to get out of there, away from school and away from everyone.

I couldn't bring myself to call my mother because then I would have to explain what happened and I didn't want to think about it anymore.

My mind turning and feelings hurt, I decided it was best to walk away from everything for a while, maybe forever. I just started walking.

I found himself heading for the downtown area and eventually, I walked right up to the pet shop….a place that gave me comfort. It was a place where I could get away from the rest of the world and I was accepted there.

I slipped inside, hoping not to be noticed. I wasn't in the mood to talk to anyone and hoped to seek a little time alone. Not seeing anyone in the front of the store, I walked quickly to the darkness of the fish room at the back of the store.

Outside the brightness of the tanks, nothing existed. It was therapeutic and an escape – kind of like when the lights are turned out at a movie theater. People immerse themselves in the story and forget about the outside world.

Similarly, I immersed myself in the underwater scenes of the aquariums. Above, fishing nets were loosely suspended from the ceiling with preserved starfish, pieces of coral, with a few hardened and shellacked blown-up pufferfish resting on the upper side of the nets. In the water, fish of every shape, size, and color danced about. They were weaving through the castles, rock formations, and the vertical stems of the colorful artificial plants. Some of the natural themed aquariums contained live plants, which had a multitude of small fish swimming among the leaves. Bubbles in each of the tanks made a kind of white noise that caused me to relax into a mildly meditative state. I wanted to stay inside with the fish, not being myself, not allowing anyone to see my red eyes from crying and certainly not talking to anyone.

I knew there must be someone managing the store, and Mitch had told me the owner grooms dogs in the back room during the day, but I was hoping no one would notice I was there—at least for a while.

I watched many of the remaining chocolate cichlids, and then I was checking out some of the clown knifefish when the back door opened. Luckily, it was Mitch, who walked into the fish room. While the door was open, I heard the hum of a hair clipper and a man mildly cursing at a dog to stand still.

"Well, hi there Peter," Mitch said. "I haven't seen you for a while. How are things going with that tank? Ready for more fish?"

"No. Not exactly," I said. "I'm happy with Chockie. I just needed to get away from school for a while."

Although Mitch and I had hardly begun to know each other, he seemed to be someone I had known for a long time. I felt I could trust Mitch enough to tell him about my troubles. I was hoping he wouldn't say anything about my wet pants or the smell of them, which he didn't.

"I see," Mitch said, rather slowly and pensively. He waited a while before talking again while I kept my eyes on the fish. "Did you see the new red terrors? They're cool." He pointed to some four-inch fish that were bright red with bright blue spots on the ends of their scales.

"Yeah," I said while looking at them moving slowly about the tank. "They are pretty neat."

"They're South American cichlids, coming from the same area of the world as your chocolate," Mitch said. "And over here, we got some pretty cool Jack Dempseys."

I was impressed with the black fish with bright blue and green dots all over their bodies. I watched them for a while. To me, the fish looked to have a sense of intelligent thought as they moved, giving me the impression that they were thinking about their next moves.

"We also got in some silver arrowanas," Mitch said, pointing to another tank. "They are pretty rare. They're kind of a prehistoric type of fish and grow big."

I looked to see several silver elongated fish with long, streaming dorsal and anal fins. The fish looked odd at the front end, with two long whiskers at the top lip, plus a trap-door mouth, hinged at the bottom, extending at an angle to the top of their heads. It reminded me of the army transport ships I'd seen, with a drop-down end gate to unload men and vehicles.

Mitch was silent for quite a while before speaking again, "So, school is not going too well right now?" Mitch asked.

"Well, you know," I said as I shrugged my shoulders. "School sucks. They make you learn all this stuff you'll never use."

Mitch didn't answer.

The silence was killing me. I thought maybe I owed him a little better explanation. Besides, I wanted someone to care, even just a little. "Did you ever have someone who constantly picked on you – for no reason…?" My voice trailed off at the end. I felt a little nervous talking about it.

"Wow," Mitch said. "Who is being mean to you?"

"This kid at school. A big, mean dumb kid."

"What do you plan to do about it?" Mitch asked.

"I'm not sure. Tell you what I'd like to do. I'd like to kill him," I said.

"Hey, hey. Let's not be thinking of something that drastic," Mitch replied. "Isn't there anything the principal or other school officials can do?"

"No..." I thought silently for a few moments. I hadn't tried everything, but then I felt ashamed of what had been done to me, and telling other people would only increase my embarrassment. In truth, I hadn't told school officials. "They won't help."

"Well, something needs to be done, if you ask me. If the principal won't help, maybe the police would," Mitch said.

"Yeah, maybe." I didn't feel like talking about it anymore.

"Hey Peter, would you like to feed the dovii? They're really fun and sometimes they'll take it right out of your fingers." Mitch grabbed a handful of mealworms from a container beneath the counter and poured them into my open hand.

One by one, I dropped them into the water and the feeding frenzy began. The dovii dashed around the tank, swallowing them, even making a loud snap at the surface as they grabbed them just as they hit the water. One fish even jumped above the water in a competitive effort to beat the other fish from getting them.

I spent a few hours with the fish and talking to Mitch, but my mind began to return to what happened earlier in the day. I began to think about what I would tell my mother about what happened at school. I was thinking maybe I shouldn't say anything.

"I better get going home," I said with a sigh when all the mealworms were gone. "I don't want to get into trouble."

Mitch dumped a dozen or so mealworms in a plastic bag and handed them to me. "Here. Feed these to Chockie. He'll like them. No charge."

I thanked him and headed out the door. I wondered if my mother would be home when I got there and what I was going to say.

CHAPTER 10
Chockie Has Something To Say

~⌒

I AVOIDED ANY CONTACT with my mother as I moved swiftly through the doorway and went straight to my room. She shouted something like "how did school go?" when I passed, but I didn't answer. I wasn't in the mood and I was afraid I'd end up crying again.

Pulling the door closed behind me, I locked the doorknob. I quickly changed my pants and threw himself on my bed with my face down in my pillow. I stayed that way, mentally wanting to escape from the world.

"What's wrong, Peter?"

I froze for a few seconds, trying to determine if what I heard was real, or just something I thought I heard. If what I heard was real, it frightened me to think someone might be in the room with me. The voice sounded like it was inside my room.

Rolling my head off the pillow, I slowly looked around the room, hoping I wouldn't see anyone. No one was within sight, so I turned sideways in the bed and hung over the side to look under the bed. A lot of junk was there, stuff I hid, but no living and breathing person there. Not even a space alien, toy, or otherwise.

I must have been hearing things, I thought, as I caught sight of Chockie in his tank, swimming excitedly at the front glass while looking back at me.

"Hi Chockie," I said. "Oh boy, you look really hungry. Do I ever have a treat for you! How would you like some mealworms?" I took out the clear plastic bag I got from the pet shop and brought it up to eye level to inspect the worms inside.

"I was more worried about you than hungry," the voice sounded again.

I heard it coming from near the fish tank and I slowly bent down to look around the ends, beneath, and behind the aquarium. "Who said that?"

"I did." Chockie stopped his waggling and suspended halfway up the glass, his eyes fixed on me.

"Chockie? That was you, Chockie?" I mumbled to myself, not believing it and joking it couldn't be Chockie saying that, but I didn't have a real explanation. "This can't be right." I kept looking behind the aquarium and on its sides for a hidden speaker. Lifting and looking under the light, I frowned.

"Someone's playing a joke on me," I said, although I could not think of anyone who would do that. Besides, no one except Mom and Dad had access to my bedroom.

"No joke, Peter, it's me."

This time the voice was near and I could tell it came from the aquarium, but I wasn't convinced it was Chockie. "No, no, no. Fish can't talk," I said, disbelieving and still thinking someone was playing a trick on me.

"When you got me from the pet shop, I swam into your bag, remember?"

I froze, unable to move as an electric shock ran through me that sent the adrenaline of fear coursing through my body. I realized no one besides me knew about Chockie swimming into the bag – that is – no one but Chockie.

Finally able to move, I ran from my room and found my mother folding clothes in her bedroom.

"Chockie talked!" I cried out. I was scared. I planned to be calm about it, but I couldn't. I felt my body tense up and I didn't know what else to say. My body began shaking.

My mom came over quickly to embrace me and gently run her hand over the hair on my head. "Okay, it's okay, Honey. Just tell me again. What has you so upset?"

"It's Chockie. He talked. I know it sounds crazy but he really did. I didn't believe it either at first. I thought someone was playing a trick on me. But he talked again and it came from the fish tank. He knew my name and everything!"

"Okay, let's go in there. I'm coming with you and we'll see."

"No, I don't want to go back in there." I held tight to the sides of her shirt into my fists.

"I'm sure it's nothing. Tell you what – I'll go in there and see what this is about. You stay here, okay?" she said. She gave me a sympathetic look.

I could tell she didn't believe me but she wanted to calm my fears. "Well … okay." I slowly let go of her shirt.

She hugged me one last time before leaving the room and going into my room.

Soon I could hear her soft voice coming from my bedroom, talking like she did to babies – a higher-pitched nonsense sort of thing. I could make out something like,

"How are you doing Chockie? Tell me about what Peter said. Did you talk to him?" I didn't hear an answer or any other voice. I waited a long time, maybe five minutes, and heard more of her coaxing Chockie to talk.

I braved myself down the hallway and peeked into my room.

She was kneeling in front of the aquarium. Her head turned and she saw me right away. "Chockie said he didn't talk to you," my mom said.

I burst out laughing and then she did, too.

My mom stayed with me while I laid on the bed and she rubbed my head until I fell asleep. I woke up when I heard Mom calling me for supper. When I was fully awake, I rolled over and sat on the edge of the bed, looking at Chockie. He was in the middle of the tank, looking back at me.

"Look, I don't know if you really can talk or not," I said sternly. "If you can, try not to scare me like that again." I let out a chuckle and then left the room for some supper.

CHAPTER 11
Calming Peter's Fears

~⁓

THE SCHOOL COUNSELOR, Mrs. Price, asked for me to
meet with her right after lunch.

For me, I found that visiting the school counselors'
office was a break from the classroom, but it wasn't a totally
enjoyable experience, especially if I had to explain a lot
of things going on in my life. I'd just rather not talk about
myself and how I felt.

"How are things going for you this week, Peter?" Mrs.
Price asked.

"Just fine," I said, avoiding eye contact by looking at the
pictures hung on the wall. The room seemed odd for being
an office, I thought. It was decorated more like a living room,
dimly lit with end tables, lamps, padded chairs, and a couch.
No matter how much I looked around the room, I always
saw something new I hadn't noticed before. It just looked so
plush like she could live here. I wondered how come she had
such a nice office and if the principal had one of these, too.

"So, have there been any bullying incidents? Have you had any contact with Ralph at all this week?"

"Um, no," I said, shifting uneasily in my chair. I would rather not talk about that stuff. Once I was in the room, I couldn't wait to get it over with. As much as I wanted to leave, I couldn't. Leaving wasn't an option.

"Nothing at all? So you have been happy all week? Classes going fine?"

"Yeah."

"I talked with your teachers and they all say that you seem distracted, that you haven't been yourself. Unfortunately, your grades haven't improved as I had hoped," Mrs. Price said, looking into my eyes. "Peter, it seems like you're uncomfortable talking to me today. Is there any reason you don't want to talk to me?"

I kept quiet and looked around the room, settling on nothing in particular.

An uncomfortable silence existed in the room for a long time.

"I'm afraid I might be going crazy," I finally said, tears forming in my eyes.

"Why do you say that? No, you're not crazy, Peter. Believe me, I know crazy when I see it and you're not crazy. My husband – now he is crazy. Why would you even think something like that?"

It took a lot for me to get the words out, but when I did, it was almost like a purging of all anguish inside me. "I'm hearing voices. I mean, not voices, I'm hearing just one voice," I said, lowering my head, ashamed and afraid what she might say next.

"When did this happen?"

"Yesterday," I answered quickly. Maybe I said too much. Probably too late to take it back.

"What did the voice tell you?" Mrs. Price asked, leaning forward as if this conversation piqued her interest.

Perhaps she never had a patient who heard a voice before, I figured. Maybe I was crazy after all. "Nothing really," I said, wishing this conversation would end and I could leave. I was getting extremely uncomfortable.

She said nothing but just waited for me to say more.

"Okay, I thought I heard a voice. I thought it was coming from Chockie, my fish. I'm not so sure now. Maybe it was just my imagination after all."

"Oh. Do you have fish? What kind of fish is he?"

"He's a chocolate cichlid. I got him from the pet shop downtown," I said.

"Chocolate cichlid. Never heard of one of those."

"Yeah. He's quite different than what most people think of when they hear the word 'fish.' He's about so big right now," I said, holding out both hands to indicate Chockie's length, "and he's kind of reddish-brown. He's really a neat fish." I felt more comfortable talking about Chockie than that other stuff.

"Wow. He does sound neat. So, what did Chockie say to you?" Mrs. Price asked, then leaned back in her chair, as if she were planning to listen to a lengthy answer.

I stared at the door with my arms crossed. I didn't want to tell her about Chockie talking. If I said any more about it, she might call in some security people and have me taken away to some mental hospital or something.

"You're not going to tell me?" she said after several minutes of awkward silence.

"He said he was concerned about me," I said while gazing at the floor. "He asked me what was wrong."

"How did you answer him?" she asked.

"I ... I'm not sure. I just got out of there," I said, not wanting to tell her how scared I'd been.

"Then what happened?" she asked. I was beginning to feel like there were too many questions. I felt exhausted in having to answer all of them.

"I told my mother and she came into my room to hear Chockie talk."

"So, did he talk to your mother?"

"No. He didn't talk at all. I swear, he talked when I was alone in my room. But then he wouldn't when she was there."

"How does that make you feel?"

I swallowed uncomfortably. "Afraid. I was afraid. It's too freaky."

"Freaky? Do you feel like you're in danger at any time?"

"Well ... no."

"He could talk to you again, but do you think Chockie could harm you in any way? Do you think he would get out of his aquarium?"

"No," I said, wiggling around in my chair. "That's silly. Fish can't live out of water." I sat silently, thinking about what I'd told Mrs. Price. I began to worry about the other kids in school finding out. "You're not going to tell anyone about this, are you?"

"No, of course not. As I told you when we first met, whatever you tell me stays between you and me. No one else will ever find out."

"Good," I said, relaxing as if I had just let down a 100-pound weight onto the floor.

"There are many stories of animals talking throughout history," she said. "For instance, in the Bible, it tells of stories where animals did talk. Remember the story of Balaam and the donkey? Remember after Balaam hit his donkey, the donkey asked, "What have I done to you to make you beat me these three times?""

I sat up straight when hearing this. She got my attention.

"Whether your fish actually talked to you or you imagined it, it shouldn't matter. Just accept it as a message to you. May I suggest something? Next time Chockie talks, maybe you should just listen to what he has to say. Don't be afraid. Just go with it. What could it hurt? I'd be interested in what he has to say. Sounds like he just wants to be your friend."

"Yeah. I suppose. He is a cool fish," I said, suddenly realizing I liked Chockie and there should be no reason to fear him. Like she said, what could it hurt to listen to him?

Time was running out, so Mrs. Price concluded our session. She told me to take note of what Chockie says, not to be afraid and similarly, and not to be afraid of Ralph. If there was trouble, I should come to the school office and tell her what happened.

As I walked out of her office, I noticed that I felt better. I didn't want to talk about my problems with her at first, but now I felt better about everything.

Before closing the door, I looked back at Mrs. Price one last time and smiled. "Thank you," I said before shutting the door, knowing my day was going to be a little bit better than the previous days.

I also was anxious to see if Chockie would talk again. Now, I kind of hoped he would talk. That would be so cool. I think.

It took a while for me to get used to a talking fish, but

after some adjustment, little by little I finally was able to talk to Chockie and have him talk back without freaking out. One day after school, I was able to let my guard down and ask him the questions I had on my mind. I was in my room and decided to ask Chockie if he was doing okay.

"I would like some of those mealworms, if you wouldn't mind," Chockie answered.

"Oh. Okay." I got the plastic bag and shuffled three worms into the palm of my hand. I lifted the lid on the tank and dropped them into the water.

Chockie immediately grabbed one in his mouth and began chewing, then moved to the bottom where the last two had landed and he quickly ate them one at a time. "Yum. Those were good. Thank you, Peter," Chockie said, now at the front glass again, looking at me.

"So, how are you able to talk? I've had you since you were a little squirt and I never heard you talk until recently." I stared at Chockie and waited for him to talk again. I was baffled by how he did it.

"Maybe I had nothing important to say. Just kidding. Do you think only humans can talk? We've been doing it since the beginning of time, or so I'm told. Don't worry about that now - I'll explain later."

"That's amazing. I saw your lips move when you talked."

"Of course my lips move. They have to. It's called breathing. You know – water in, water out. What's going on with you? You seem upset."

"I had a rough day. I have to see a counselor now, all because of Ralph," I said, tears welling up in my eyes and fighting hard not to cry. "And now I'm talking to a fish. I don't believe it. My life sucks."

"Hey! For your information, I'm not just an ordinary

pond fish. I'm your friend," Chockie said, maintaining a still position by constantly rotating his pectoral fins.

"What would you know ..." I snapped back, but then instantly regretted it. "I'm sorry, Chockie. I'm going through a lot right now, including trying to believe you can talk. Fish can't talk."

"I can. You hear me now, don't you?" Chockie asked. After several seconds, Chockie broke the silence, "I care about you, Peter. I care about you and what you're going through. You're my best friend."

I stood silent for a minute. "Okay. What do you suggest? I don't want to go to school again and I most definitely don't want to see that Ralph ever again. I wish I didn't get so confused at times. When Ralph picks on me, I just freeze. I can't think straight and I can't react fast enough. Then later I think about what I should have done."

"Believe it or not, fish also have bullies. You can either fight or swim away. Those are the only two options we have. We may lose some scales, but we heal and keep on swimming."

"That doesn't help."

"Maybe you need to swim more and fight less. You know, do your own thing, and don't let that bully make your life so miserable. Do what you like to do, do it often, and forget about him. Don't let the past ruin your present."

"Sounds good in theory, but I can't control when he wants to ruin my present."

"Then, go to the source. Ask him why he is so mean to you. Find out. Ask him what could be done to make it stop. The worst part of your worries is not knowing why."

"I guess you are right," I said, but in my mind, I would rather just avoid Ralph and whatever he had to say to me. Talking to him would be rather unpleasant, to say the least.

My stomach growled. I realized I didn't eat lunch again and now it was catching up with me. I could hear my mother making supper in the kitchen. Perhaps I could get something, even if it was a snack. I headed toward the door, but then stopped suddenly. I took a couple of steps back so I could see Chockie. "I'll be right back. Don't go anywhere."

"Where would I go? I'm in a fish tank."

I walked softly to the kitchen, peering before entering to see my mother chopping up some potatoes on the cutting board.

As soon as I stepped fully into the room, my mother turned her head. "So, you came out of your cave to join the rest of the world?" she asked.

"Yeah."

"That's great. Your father will be home in a few minutes and supper is almost done," she said, turning her head toward me while she stirred something sizzling in the frying pan. "How was school today?"

"Fine," I said, sitting down on a chair at the table. By the familiar odor emanating from the frying pan, I could tell she was preparing pork again for supper, most likely pork chops because it was my father's favorite meal – and mashed potatoes with some vegetable like green beans or peas, which were probably in the other two pans on the stove. I didn't mind pork chops again, but I didn't like vegetables.

"Well, don't talk so much. I can hardly keep up with you," my mother said sarcastically. She must've seen that I was feeling down. "Are you keeping up with your homework? If you need some help, just say so. I can help you as much as I can."

"Thanks, Mom, but I'm doing okay. I'm all caught up on my assignments."

She turned to look at my face.

I turned my gaze to avoid looking at her.

"Peter? What's wrong?" she asked, setting a spatula in the spoon rest on top of the stove. She came over to squat and look me in my eyes. "Is it those bullies on the bus again?"

"No Mom."

"Because if it is, I'll go back to that office and demand that they are thrown off the bus. I won't tolerate such behavior. I was bullied when I was in school and I wouldn't put up with it."

"Yeah?" I lifted my head and looked at her. "What happened? What did you do?"

"There were these girls – you know how girls can be – who teased me because I wasn't part of their group. They thought I looked plain. Girls are all about looks and what guys they can attract. Well, they called me homely because they thought I was unattractive."

"So, how did you stop it?"

"I didn't. When the captain of the football team asked me to the junior prom, they stopped. I guess they couldn't compete with that."

"Really? The captain of the football team asked you out?"

"Yeah, he did. He's your father."

"Oh wow," I said, a smile breaking out on my face.

"So, don't think it's the end of the world if someone doesn't like you. As you grow older, you'll find that everyone has someone who doesn't like them, for whatever odd reason. Maybe one day, you won't like someone, too. Maybe you do now."

"Well, yeah. Maybe."

"Bad times never last, Peter. Keep that in mind. Just when you think everything is terrible and it's the darkest time in your life, suddenly something happens and life is good again. Don't give up when bad things happen. You'll be glad you held on for the good times."

My mother and I turned our heads when we heard the door to the garage opening. A little later we saw my dad walk into the house.

"Hi Honey," Mom called over to him. She rose and walked in his direction as he took off his jacket and hat. "How was your day?"

"The same," he said flatly, hanging his coat and hat on the wooden pegs in the hallway. His eyes darted between me and my mother, looking suspicious as if he walked in on the middle of something. "Something smells good." His attention suddenly went to what was on the stove.

I stayed in the kitchen while my father walked into his bedroom and changed his clothes. He came out to wash his hands in the kitchen sink while my mother continued to monitor the food on the stove. I figured I might as well sit tight because supper would be on soon and I'd just have to come back anyway. Besides, I didn't want to break the connection between me and my mother.

I sat at the kitchen table. My forefinger traced the gouges in the wooden tabletop, now well-worn but as familiar as an old friend. I remembered the day I accidentally made those grooves in the table. One of my hobbies was model rocketry when I was younger and I was cutting fins of balsa wood with an X-Acto knife. I didn't realize I was cutting through the balsa wood, the newspapers below, and made some serious cuts into the table. My father was furious at the time, but the grooves became a common sight and part of our family, and the topic was never discussed again. The anger and embarrassment faded then eventually, the grooves became familiar. They were now part of our memories and part of our lives.

My father sat down at the head of the table, as he always did, with me and my mother sitting on either side. The conversation from my father was usually about his job and how the people at work made him upset.

After supper, I retreated to my room and blocked the gap beneath the door with a couple of towels, then I jumped onto the bed, facing the fish tank. "Hi Chockie," I said. I kept thinking about what Mom had just told me and it had lifted my spirits. "I'm back."

"I can see that. Where did you go?"

"Just to supper. By chance – are you hungry?"

"Yes. I'm always hungry. But I would like something different than what you've been giving me."

"Like what?"

"Do you have any shrimp? Or maybe some worms? I love worms."

"Not at the moment. You already ate the last of the mealworms, but I can get you some more. Not sure about shrimp though. I'm pretty sure we don't have any," I said. "If you can wait, I'll see what I can get tomorrow at the pet shop."

"Okay."

I sat quietly, looking at Chockie while Chockie looked back at me.

"Do you get lonely? I mean, you are here alone all day while I'm at school. Would you like me to get another fish to keep you company?"

"No, I don't get very lonely. I'm not a schooling fish. My kind of fish just spends its day in solitude, foraging, and snapping at bugs on the surface. I don't get lonely, but I do get bored. There isn't much to do when you're not here."

"Maybe I can figure out something for you to do," I said, putting my fist to my lips in thought. "Could you do my homework?"

"No, Peter. You have to do that yourself. Besides, there's no way I can hold a pencil."

"Oh, all right," I said. "Looks like I'll have to do it myself. Maybe you can give some advice about geometry."

"Not a chance," Chockie said. "Triangles and squares are not my things."

CHAPTER 12
Just Chockie and Tommy

~

I WOKE UP THE next morning with a new sense of purpose and optimism. After rushing to eat some cereal and get dressed, I said my farewells to Chockie, then my mother, and headed out to catch the bus. On my way, I wondered if Chockie would ever talk to anyone else – maybe my mother since he already knew her. I wondered if that might happen while Mom was home and I was in school. I also wondered how she might react.

I shut this thought out of my mind and went to the end of the driveway to wait for the bus. The bus came and I climbed up the steps. Luckily, Ralph was still serving his sentence up in front, so the trip was safe.

When the bus arrived at school and the kids got off, I immediately looked for Tommy. I found him in the hallway near his locker and I asked him to go into the bathroom so we could talk in private. Luckily, no one else was there.

"Remember what you were telling me about how the animals used to talk?" I asked, rather excited about what

I was about to tell him. I was going to keep in a secret, but now I couldn't wait to tell him.

"Yeah. But that was a long time ago. What about it?"

"Could that happen again? I mean, do all the animals know how to talk with us, just that they choose not to? Could they do it again if they wanted?" I asked.

"Not sure. Are you okay? You're acting a little weird right now."

"What you said is true. Animals can talk. My Chockie did yesterday. I still can't get over it. It's incredible."

"Wait ... what is Chockie?"

"I'm telling you – Chockie, my fish, talked. He talked a lot - not just repeating stuff. We talked to each other – like in a conversation."

"Come on, man. Are you sure? Someone must have been playing a joke on you."

"That's what I thought too, but he told me stuff only he could know. Honest, Tommy. I swear to God. I'm not making this stuff up."

The door flew open and a couple of boys stepped into the bathroom, breaking our conversation.

"I'll talk to you about this later," I said, then exited the door with Tommy behind. I wasn't about to talk about this while other kids could hear. Even I thought it sounded crazy.

"Yeah. Maybe I can stop at your house after school," Tommy said as we walked down the hallway.

"Cool. See ya then."

Classes went slowly for me. I wished I could speed up time so I could get back home to Chockie. I felt anxious to show Tommy what Chockie could do. In most of my classes, I hardly listened to the teacher at all. Instead, I drew pictures of Chockie all over the pages of my notebook.

When the final bell rang, I waited outside the school building as everyone walked past me to the waiting buses on the street. When Tommy finally joined up with me, we got on my bus, first clearing it with the bus driver, and rode to my house.

When we filed through the front door, my mother was surprised to see Tommy walking behind me.

"Tommy came over to see Chockie. He's never seen him," I said. Maybe Chockie talked to her, I wondered. I thought she would say something if Chockie talked to her. It wouldn't be something she would keep to herself, I figured. If Chockie were to talk to Mom, I would be glad it would be her and not Dad. I'm not sure how he would react, but I'm betting it wouldn't be good.

We walked into the bedroom and Tommy's eyes immediately became fixed on the aquarium and my fish. Chockie came to the front of the glass, saw me, but then he saw Tommy and dashed behind the plastic plants and rocks.

"What's wrong with him?" Tommy asked.

"I think he got scared. He's never seen you before," I said. "Sit down here and try not to move suddenly. He'll come out once he gets used to you."

We sat on the edge of the bed and waited.

"What is the matter, Chockie? Come on out, Tommy wants to see you," I pleaded.

Chockie remained elusive and peeked from behind obstacles in his aquarium.

I dropped some food on the top of the water in an attempt to break him from his cover, but he stayed hidden. "Come on out, Chockie. It's me…Peter."

Chockie wouldn't budge.

For the next 15 minutes, we remained sitting and trying

to provoke Chockie to at least come out into the open, but nothing we tried would work. None of the food I'd placed in the tank was touched or even looked at by Chockie.

"Well, I better get going," Tommy said in resignation. "By the time I get home, my parents will be wondering what happened to me."

I could tell Tommy had enough waiting and was a little skeptical about Chockie talking, but perhaps he didn't want to hurt my feelings. Maybe he even thought I was crazy.

"Yeah. I'm sorry, Tommy. I don't understand what got into him. Maybe once he gets to know you, he'll show you."

"Yeah, maybe. Don't worry about it. Fish are funny that way," Tommy said. "I'll see you tomorrow at school. Maybe you can tell me more about it then. I got to get going."

Tommy walked through the house and toward the front door when my mother asked if he would like to stay for supper. When he declined, she offered him a ride home. He agreed, so they left, with me preferring to stay behind.

Once I went back into my bedroom, Chockie came out and remained at the front glass, looking at me.

"What happened, Chockie? That was my friend, Tommy. Why did you hide the entire time?" I tried to remain calm, but I was a little upset. "I wanted to show him that you talked. Now he'll never believe anything I say."

"I'm sorry," Chockie said. "I didn't mean to hurt your feelings."

"But why did you hide, then?"

"He is a stranger. I don't know him."

I gave out a sigh and stood silent for a few seconds.

"I only trust you, Peter."

This last line hit me hard because I knew that was how I felt, too. I had a few friends, especially Tommy, but none

I could trust to tell everything. I trusted Chockie completely and now I felt bad for becoming disappointed with him. "I'm sorry, Chockie. I shouldn't have surprised you with that," I managed to say, trying to fight back the tears welling in my eyes.

"I let you down," Chockie said.

"No, no. I let *you* down. You trusted me to keep this between us and I betrayed your trust. From now on, it's just us. Okay?"

Chockie paused for a moment and then said, "Okay."

Later that evening, I listened to the radio while doing my homework. I was figuring out some math problems, tapping my pencil on the paper, when I began singing loudly to the song.

Chockie made a big splash, sending water flying from every gap in the aquarium cover.

"What was that all about?" I asked.

"That noise you made – it surprised me."

"What noise? What are you talking about?"

"You know – that 'heeba - jeeba' thing," Chockie said.

I tried to figure out what he was talking about when it suddenly dawned on me. "Oh, you mean my singing?"

"I don't know what you call it, but there was a bunch of noise coming out of your mouth and it didn't sound like words."

"I was singing, Chockie. I was singing along to the song on the radio."

Chockie fell silent for several seconds. "So, what purpose does that serve?"

"It makes me happy. It's a way to express happiness, sort of like dancing."

"Oh, now I know what dancing is," Chockie said. "We do it all the time when we are happy." Chockie exaggeratedly wiggled his body while swimming from one end of the tank to the other. Then he stopped at the front glass and looked at me again. "I know dancing. But I don't know what it was you were doing. Sounded kind of like a distress call to me."

"No. It's singing. It makes people happy to sing. You ought to try it."

"Eeeeeee rrrrrrrrrrrrrrrrrrrrrr!" Chockie screamed.

"No, no, no. On second thought, you better skip that. Maybe dancing is your talent."

A knock sounded on the door.

"Peter. Are you okay in there?"

"Yeah, Mom."

The door swung open.

"I heard noises in here. Is everything okay?" Her eyes darted around the room, looking for possible sources of the disturbance.

"No one else in here, Mom. Just Chockie and me. Maybe you heard Chockie singing," I said with a smirk on my face, knowing she wouldn't take me seriously.

"I must be losing my mind," she said under her breath as she turned and left the room, pulling the door shut behind her.

"Good one," Chockie said. "'Just Chockie and me,' you said. I don't think she believed you."

CHAPTER 13
A Difficult Situation

~⌒

C HOCKIE'S SIZE GREW to about a foot in length, to the point I was beginning to think his tank was too small for him. Chockie didn't complain, but I knew it was getting rather cramped.

I felt sorry for Chockie, who was stuck being indoors all the time, so I began to think of something I could do for him. I was thinking he was outgrowing his tank. I had all my hopes on a bigger aquarium.

"Mom, do you think that maybe I could get a larger tank for Chockie? He's grown a lot and he's cramped," I asked. "Mitch told me I could trade in the tank I got for a used 55-gallon tank he has down at the pet shop."

"Is there enough room in your bedroom? Where are you going to get the money? We have enough trouble paying the bills and I'm not sure a bigger tank is such a good idea."

"I've been keeping his tank clean, just like I promised. There's plenty of room for it. I just might have to rearrange a few things, that's all. Please?" I pleaded. "Mitch said I could help him clean tanks at the pet shop and bag up some rabbit food and stuff. I could get some money that way."

"Well, I don't know. I might have to talk to your father about this. Not sure he'd like it."

"Let me show you how well I can work. I'll even do chores for you. I'll even clean my room." Cleaning my room was always a big issue for her and I figured if I promised to keep my room clean, that might seal the deal.

"Okay. I'll let you work at the pet shop on a trial basis, but just for a few hours a week. We'll see after that. But not a word about it to your father until I can talk to him. Understand?"

I began working at the pet shop on Tuesdays and Thursdays after school. On some days, I would have to net the fish out of a couple of aquariums, drain the water into a sink with a hose, and then carry the tank to the back room. There, I removed and washed the gravel, scrubbed the inside of the glass with a sponge to remove algae, then put back the gravel and placed it back on the rack in the fish room. After filling the tanks with water, I added some water conditioner and allowed the water to aerate and exchange gasses. Fish would be added back to the tank the next day when the water had properly aged and adjusted.

When I wasn't cleaning tanks, I would have to clean small animal cages up in front of the store or the bird cages in the bird room, which I considered the worst job. Inside the bird room, the canaries, finches, and parrots would excitedly fly around and stir up all the bird dust. The dust would make breathing difficult, not to mention the constant loud squawking, which hurt my ears. The trays would need to be removed and a new newspaper installed, then water and food replenished.

Overall, I enjoyed my job and I couldn't wait to get there after school. Mitch spoke to the owner and it was agreed to pay me $7 an hour, which I hoped would add up soon and allow me to buy the 55-gallon tank. However, that wasn't the only expense, since I also needed a top and light, a larger heater, and a bigger filter to handle the additional load and water volume.

I often took extra time making the fish tanks look good. Most tanks I had seen at pet shops were bare, except for the fish and gravel, which made catching the fish with a net much easier. But that didn't look right and I thought the fish never felt comfortable, just swimming in open water and having nothing to swim through and behind.

I began studying the natural environments for each species of fish and tried to duplicate them, whether it was rocky caves and crevices, or planted underwater landscapes.

"Don't you think you're going overboard with those tanks?" Mitch would ask me. "I mean, most of the time we have to tear them apart to get at the fish."

"I suppose. I just want them to feel at home - you know - as if they belong there. They need their little places to live and feel comfortable," I said.

Mitch said it was okay, although maybe it was a little more than necessary, mainly because I was thinking of Chockie and I knew that sort of thing made him happy.

I knew the home environment for African cichlids was rock structures of caves and passageways so they could swim through the holes and graze algae from the surfaces. One day, I brought in several boxes of flat rocks I had collected along a local riverbed, then cleaned and sterilized them. I assembled a maze of rocks by stacking them precisely in a 55-gallon tank in the fish room. The variety of bright cobalt blue, canary yellow, purple, and orange fish darting and dashing around the tank was an eye-catching natural environment that seized everyone's attention.

Mitch was impressed.

I made it a habit of walking from the school to the pet shop for work every Tuesday and Thursday after school, something that apparently hadn't gone unnoticed.

One afternoon, I noticed a group of four boys following me down the sidewalk. I noticed they walked faster and were gaining on me, so I quickened my pace. The boys behind me did too This got to the point where I and all of them were running at a full sprint. Main Street was ahead of me another block and I figured I'd be safe if I could make it to the pet shop before they did.

I glanced both ways as I neared Main Street and decided I could make it without any interference with cars. My heart was pounding loudly, my arms pumping hard, and I didn't break stride as I bounded across the blacktop.

My eyes were glued to the front door of the pet shop as I heard the footsteps and the heavy breathing directly behind me. Just as I thought I could make it, my foot caught on the curb. I lost my balance and fell onto the sidewalk, my hands scraping on the concrete.

Two of the boys stood above me.

"Where do you think you're going, Petey?" one of them said, puffing while trying to catch his breath.

I recognized the voice as Shawn. I squinted against the sunlight to confirm that it was Shawn along with Mark.

I picked myself up and stood in the center.

Someone approached from behind and the boys parted for him. It was Ralph. Since he was bigger than the others, he couldn't run as fast. "So, you got yourself a job, did ya,

Petey?" Ralph said. "What, do you get to play with the hermit crabs?"

The other boys laughed loudly.

Ralph grabbed my shirt near my neck and twisted it tightly, pushing me up against the pet store window. "Listen, you little punk. You got me into a lot of trouble after you tattled on me," he shouted with spit splattering in my face. "You don't ever say another word to anyone about me, you understand?"

Suddenly, the door from the pet shop swung open and Mitch stepped out, grabbing Ralph's left arm. "What's going on out here?" Mitch yelled. "You get your hands off Peter or I'll break them!"

Ralph let go of me and backed away while the other two boys took off.

"This ain't over, Petey! I'll never forget what you did!" Ralph yelled, then turned and trotted to follow where the other boys had gathered across the street.

Mitch helped me into the store while glancing at the boys as we went through the doorway. "Are you okay?" He bent his knees slightly while looking into my eyes.

"Yeah." I turned my head and looked away, too embarrassed to say what I was thinking. "I'm okay. I just want to get to work." I walked toward the back room, hoping to forget what just happened, even though the confrontation was so overwhelming, I couldn't think about anything else.

I immediately went to work and avoided Mitch, not wanting to talk about the incident. I began netting fish in one of the aquariums due to be cleaned. I could sense Mitch behind me, so I turned to see him with his hands on his hips. I could tell what was coming next.

"So, are you going to talk about it or not?" Mitch asked me sternly. He was waiting for my answer.

"I'd rather not," I answered softly.

"You know if you don't do something – if you don't even tell anyone about it – everything will remain the same. You'll be running from it for the rest of your life."

"Yeah. I know. I just don't want to deal with it right now."

"Well, I guess you need some time to think about this one, but don't let it go. You need to do something about it. I'll help you, Peter. I know you're embarrassed about it, but you'll go on being embarrassed every time this stuff happens. It could get much worse. What if you or someone gets hurt - seriously hurt?"

His words began to sink in.

It was a few minutes before he spoke again, "I know what it's like," Mitch's voice softened. "I was bullied, too, when I was in school."

A shock ran through me when I heard this. To me, Mitch was a cool guy, someone who I thought everyone would have respected and admired. I immediately stopped what I was doing, one hand on the net, the other grasping the edge of the tank, as I turned to look directly at Mitch for the first time since the incident outside the pet shop.

"Yeah, that's right," Mitch said. "It's not fun, having to worry about where you go because who might be there. Then you have to worry about who might see you being bullied and what they might say about you. And the biggest worry is that your parents might find out what happened – that's the worse part. It's painful."

Mitch's words were just like they were taken out of my mind, I thought. "So, what do I do?"

"I didn't handle it very well, either, when I was young," Mitch said. "I was afraid to tell anyone, too, at first. But then I got tired of hiding, so one day I went to the police department and told them what was going on."

"The police? Wow. I don't want to go through that. My dad would hit the roof."

"They turned it over to social services, who contacted the school. The kids who were teasing me weren't allowed to go anywhere near me."

"Did your parents find out?"

"Yeah, but they were okay with it. It turns out that they wanted to help me."

"I'm not so sure my dad would take it very well. I'd rather not have him know what is happening. He'd tell me to grow up or something."

"Aw, yeah. I can see that would be a problem. But you have to do something about this. If you want, I'll close up the shop and we'll go down to the police station right now."

I frowned, not liking the idea. "Give me some time to think about it."

"Okay. But don't think about it too long," Mitch said. He began to walk away when he suddenly stopped. "What did that boy mean by, 'I'll never forget what you did'?"

I lowered my head and stared at the floor. "I don't know," I said. "I'm not sure."

I spent the rest of the late afternoon cleaning tanks, then feeding and watering the small animals and birds. When it was time to go, Mitch offered to give me a ride home. "Why don't we take the 55-gallon tank along?" Mitch offered. "I know you'll work off the rest of it, so let's get it up and running. I'm sure Chockie will appreciate it."

"Okay," I said, getting more hyped the more I thought about it.

We each grabbed an end of the 55-gallon tank, which

was heavier than it looked, and loaded it into the backseat of Mitch's brown Taurus.

Mitch went into the back room and returned with the used filter and a heater, then placed them carefully on the floor of the backseat area. "So, what you think?" Mitch asked on the drive.

"I'm excited," I replied. "I can't wait to get it going. I can't wait to see the look on Chockie's face."

"Oh. Yeah. I kind of meant about the thing with Ralph. Are you going to tell anybody?"

"I'll probably tell my mom. Maybe. I don't think she'll say anything to Dad. At least, I hope not."

"Well, that's good. Keep in mind, I'll help you however I can." Mitch drove into my driveway.

Now, my excitement stepped up a notch. As soon as the car came to a stop, I got out and ran into the house to alert my mother that the tank had made its arrival. I quickly headed to my room to make room for it between the side of my bed and the outside wall.

Mitch caught up with me in my room and he said there wasn't enough time to get the tank running tonight. Besides, I needed a larger stand, and Mitch said he'd bring it tomorrow.

I felt a little disappointed, but I understood.

Mitch left the room to get some things from the car, but when I later left to go help him, I found Mitch and my mother talking to each other. I suddenly became frightened that Mitch might talk about what had happened with Ralph and me earlier in the day.

"He's a dedicated worker," I overheard Mitch telling my mother. "I'm glad he's working for us. I enjoy having him there." He smiled and turned to look at me, then turn back to face my mom. "That way, I can take it easy while he does all the dirty work."

My mom laughed.

Mitch nodded his head to the right while looking at me. "Should we get it unloaded?"

"Yeah. Let's do it."

I took the back end of the tank while Mitch held the front end while walking into the house, down the hallway, and maneuvered it through my bedroom door. We deposited on the floor near the closet where I'd cleared a place. I then turned to Chockie and smiled.

"Chockie, this is Mitch. I figure you don't remember him, but he runs the pet shop where I got you." Then I turned to Mitch and waved my hand toward the tank, palm up, and said, "Mitch, this is Chockie, the greatest fish ever to inhabit the earth."

Mitch put one hand on his stomach, the other on his back, and bowed. "It is both an honor and a privilege to meet you, Sir Chockie."

A broad grin broke out on my face.

"Wow. He sure has grown," Mitch said. "I can see why you want to give him a bigger tank. I don't think I've ever seen a chocolate cichlid this big. You must feed him well."

Chockie had grown to about 13 inches long, but he also was getting stocky and had grown a pronounced hump on his head, a sign of maturity in a male chocolate cichlid, I learned while reading about them.

Chockie swam back and forth in the tank, almost as if he were showing off to Mitch.

"Look at him go!" Mitch smiled, amazed at how proud and handsome Chockie had become. "You have a real prize fish there, Peter. That's because of your TLC, I'm sure."

Having to head home, Mitch said he could come over after school the next day to make the aquarium swap, then he headed out the door.

I stood for a second, watching Chockie, and then dashed through my doorway. "Mitch!" I called after him. Mitch was at the end of the hallway when he heard me.

He turned around.

"Mitch," I said. "Thank you."

He pointed his index finger toward me, pretending to pull the trigger and the gun going off, the kick causing his finger to point toward the ceiling. A grin formed on his face. "No problem. See you tomorrow."

CHAPTER 14
Chockie Gets a Bigger Tank

~⌒

M ITCH CAME OVER after I returned from school, just as he promised, spending part of his day off work to help me.

We cleaned and rinsed out the 55-gallon aquarium then washed some gravel Mitch had brought along and placed it into the tank. I removed all the ornaments in Chockie's aquarium. Then we siphoned some of the water into plastic pails and one plastic storage tote.

When the water was sufficiently high in the plastic storage tote, Mitch turned to me. "It's time."

I gulped. I knew what had to be done, but I didn't like doing it. It was scary. I had to move Chockie from the aquarium to the tote as fast and painless as possible. I knew Chockie wouldn't like being out of the water very long, but it could be dangerous, I thought.

I didn't want to use a net. With fish as large as Chockie, some severe damage could occur to the fish when using a net, especially to the eyes and scales. For this reason, I went to the bathroom and returned with a white bath towel. I squatted down in front of the tank to discuss the procedure with my friend, "Chockie, I need to move you to that tub so we can get your new tank ready. Now, please don't freak out. I'm going to move you fast with this towel. It won't hurt a bit." I held out the towel so Chockie could see it.

I stood up and gently laid the towel on the top of the water so it could soak up water. When it did, the towel began to sink slowly into the tank and eventually came down lightly on top of Chockie. I placed my hands on top of the towel and moved on both sides of Chockie with it, moving it down until the towel was fully wrapped around him.

I gently lifted the towel-shrouded Chockie from the tank and swiftly moved to the tote, where I immersed Chockie, towel, and all. After a few seconds, I removed the towel to see Chockie upright, gills moving, fins waving, and, overall, doing fine.

Mitch retrieved an air pump, airline, and air stone from his car and placed the air stone in the storage tote to circulate the water. He also placed the heater from the 30-gallon tank in the water to maintain the correct temperature.

We moved quickly to siphon out the rest of the water from the tank and remove the tank from the stand.

He brought with him a different stand, one a little longer to fit the bigger tank. He said he was making an even-up exchange for my smaller one, but I knew he was doing me a huge favor. The bigger stand was put into place, which made it rather cramped in my small bedroom. We put it on the far side of my bed, along the outside wall.

We positioned the 55-gallon tank on the stand, hung the filter on the back, and placed the heater inside. Mitch began lifting the plastic pails and pouring the water into the tank.

I would have done it, but raising that much water to the top rim of the tank was a little more than I could lift.

After Mitch emptied all the buckets, I got a step-stool to place the driftwood and plastic plants into the new tank.

Mitch then added fresh water up until the point where the filter could begin sucking in water and returning it to the tank in a crashing waterfall. The submersible heaters were plugged in to begin heating the water temperature properly. "There. We'll let it circulate a little longer to get the water oxygenated."

In the meanwhile, we rinsed the gravel from the old tank and placed it into the new one.

"You don't want to clean the gravel too much," Mitch said. "We want to keep the good bacteria in there, so they can begin growing and doing their job in the new setup."

I scrubbed out the 30-gallon tank, dried it with some towels, and put it in the back seat of Mitch's car. I grabbed the aquarium top and light for the 55-gallon tank, and then returned to my room.

"It's been circulating for a while, so we can probably top off the tank, check the temperature and put Chockie back," Mitch said.

The temperature was a perfect 80 degrees, so I began the delicate procedure of laying the towel over Chockie and transferring him to his new home.

After I released him and pulled out the towel, I was anxious to see if he liked his new environment. "There you go, Chockie," I said. "What do you think?" I could tell he was stressed.

Chockie's color looked washed out – a pale brown with pronounced black spots on his side. Chockie sat at the bottom of the tank, not moving and breathing rather rapidly. His color changed with his moods – darker brown when happy and feeling good and lighter brown when stressed.

But I had never seen these colors before. He was the lightest color I had ever seen him. "Mitch!" I think something is wrong!" I was panicking.

Mitch came over and peered into the tank, looking at Chockie's lethargic attitude in the water. "Just give him some time. He's stressed from being moved, the fresh water we added, plus he's in a new tank. He'll be okay."

I stood back with my hand cupped over my mouth, not saying a word while I stared at Chockie.

We stood and waited for several minutes before Chockie slowly rose to the surface.

His color began to darken and his eyes turned in every direction, looking over his new tank.

I let out a huge sigh and a slight smile.

"Okay, I am pretty sure he'll be alright," Mitch said. He could see how much I had been frightened. "I got to get going, so I'm going to leave the rest to you. Trust me. He'll be okay."

"Thank you so much, Mitch," I said. "This will be great. I know Chockie will love it. Ain't that right, Chockie?"

The fish turned and faced us at the front glass as if he were reassuring us that his world was good again.

CHAPTER 15

Peter Uncovers a Painful Past

⁓

EVERAL WEEKS PASSED and Chockie continued to grow. Frequently, I would bring home a treat from the pet store and Chockie would gobble up everything that entered his tank. Sometimes Mitch would let me have some treats for free, at other times, when the treats were more expensive, Mitch would put them on a tab for me. I was determined to repay the store somehow, along with the money I owed for the 55-gallon aquarium.

As the weather began to turn warmer, spring turned into summer and I began to spend more time outdoors. One Saturday I saw my mother raking leaves and doing other yard chores. The weather seemed to be good, in the 70s and sunshine.

"I could do a few chores around here, too," I said to Mom. "Is there anything I can do?"

"Well, now that's an idea. The garage is a mess and I've been meaning to clean it out, but I never seem to have the time."

"Yeah. I can do that. Let me show you I can do a good job." I started toward the garage, but she suddenly called to me.

"That's quite a big job to do by yourself. Why don't you ask Tommy to help you? I'll pay him, too."

I went into the house and called Tommy. He agreed to help, plus it was an opportunity to horse around together. Mom and I went to his house and picked him up.

Many years of collecting things had cluttered up the garage and it needed cleaning badly. My dad had to work that day, so I figured we would surprise him by making the garage clean.

We began by dragging out much of the larger items onto the driveway, such as the push lawn mower, bicycles, and garden tools. A large plastic garbage can began to fill up with scraps from various projects. My dad tinkers with doing his own car maintenance, so there was a multitude of worn-out car parts in various places around the building.

Along the back wall of the garage, stacked to the ceiling, were two rows of plastic totes.

"What's in these?" Tommy asked.

"I don't know," I said. "They've been there forever. I think they're just papers, clothes and stuff. I saw my mom go in there a couple of times."

"Well, let's move them outside, so we can sweep this place out."

We began trying to slide a whole stack of them along the floor, but the job became difficult and the top totes were swaying to the point that they were about to fall over. Tommy climbed up the stepladder, took the totes from the top, and handed them to me, then I set them on the floor. When they were positioned all over the floor, we began taking them outside and placed them on the lawn and driveway.

Tommy snapped the lid off one of the blue totes and peered inside. I saw the puzzled look on his face and came over to look. Inside were stuffed animals, such as a teddy bear, a puppy, and a rabbit. Some girls' clothes also were inside and on the top were some framed pictures wrapped in a lightweight white paper. I picked one up and unwrapped it.

It was a posed picture of a little girl in front of a gray muslin background, blond hair, and a big smile on her face. She wore a white dress and had a white ribbon in her hair. She appeared to be about 12 years old.

"Who is that?" Tommy asked.

My eyes were glued to the image. I didn't speak for a long time. "I don't know," I finally said. I held the frame with both hands while looking at the image when the front door swung open.

"Peter!" my mother exclaimed when she saw what was going on. "Why are you going through that stuff? You put that back!"

I froze. I couldn't imagine why she was so upset. "Who is this?" I asked, staring at the photo and then turning to look at my mother.

"Wow," she said. "You weren't supposed to see this. I just couldn't part with any of it." Tears began to well up in her eyes.

"What? What do you mean? Mom?" A sense of shock began to filter through my body as if I had discovered something dreadful. I was just as worried about the sorrow in my mother's voice and the way she was reacting.

"I don't know how to tell you this," she said, tears now freely flowing down her cheeks. She took one side of the frame with one hand and pointed with her index finger on her other hand at the picture of the little girl. "This is Sarah. She was your sister."

I couldn't comprehend what I just heard. I looked in my mother's eyes, searching for more. "What do you mean? I don't have a sister." Although it was a statement, it came out more of a question. This was a big shock and I knew it couldn't be true.

She took the photo and set it back into the tote, then wrapped her arms around me. She began sobbing. "Sarah was your sister. She died when you were a baby."

I let those words soak in. She was about the age I was now. I felt some guilt, knowing I should feel sad, but I never knew her, so it was difficult for me to grasp those emotions. Mostly, I felt sorrow for my mother, who was very shaken. "What happened? I mean, how did she die?" I looked back down to the photograph in the tote, both to try to see if she looked familiar to me and to avert my eyes from my mother, whose sobbing was beginning to make me well up in tears.

"It was an accident. She—died in a car accident. Your father was driving. Well—it was bad. Let's not talk about this right now." She suddenly looked at Tommy, who had retreated to the doorway of the garage, watching everything unfold. Wiping the tears from her eyes with her hand, she backed up a few steps. "You boys—just go ahead and finish what you were doing…" Displaying her palms in a pushing motion towards the totes then she turned and walked back into the house.

Tommy and I stood motionless, glancing at each other, wondering what to do. The sense of unease was broken when Tommy picked up a shop broom and began sweeping the garage floor. I wrapped the framed photograph with the paper, placed it back in the tote, and snapped the lid down tight.

We continued to sweep, throwing out a multitude of junk and started to reorganize as we began to place the items back. We didn't talk much and our work was just a way to think through what had just happened. There were several hooks in a bag, never used, so we mounted them on the wall for bicycles and other items to be neatly hung there.

"In Ho-Chunk culture, a baby doesn't belong to the parents until it reaches 4 years old," Tommy said out of the blue.

I could see that Tommy cared and he was trying to comfort me. "Until the baby reaches 4, it still belongs to the Creator and He can take it back at any time. Once it is 4, then it belongs to the parents."

"Wow. I never heard of such a weird thing," I said, knowing he was trying to make me feel better, but it wasn't helping much at the moment. "Sarah was older than that."

"Yeah," Tommy said. "Yeah. I know. I'm sorry."

When we were all done cleaning and putting things away, Tommy said he had to get going, so he said goodbye to me, and Mom took him home.

I avoided talking to my mother when she came back. I felt a little awkward about the new development, learning about a sister I never knew, and I wanted to avoid talking about it for a while. It wasn't a pleasant feeling.

In my bedroom, I shut the door and threw a few treats into the water for Chockie.

"Hi Peter," Chockie said.

"Hi, Chockie," I said dejectedly, flopping myself onto my bed. I buried my face into my pillow.

"You don't look very happy. Anything wrong?"

I raised my head. "Yeah. I found out I once had a sister. She died."

Chockie was silent. "She died just now?" he asked.

"No. No. No. She died when I was a baby. I don't remember her at all…" My voice tapered off. "I wish I did remember her. I wish I could have her around now. I wish she never died."

"I'm sorry."

"No, it's not your fault, Chockie. They never told me. They never told me I had a sister. They never told me she died. Why did they keep that from me? It's not fair."

"Maybe they saw no reason to put you through the sorrow. Maybe they thought you were too young to understand all of it."

"Yeah. Maybe," I said. "I'm old enough to understand now. They could have told me."

Just before supper, I went into the kitchen while my mother was making something on the stove.

She laid the spatula down and went to her purse. She reached in, took out her wallet, and pulled out a $10 bill, and handed it to me. "Here's for the work you did today. I already gave Tommy one when I took him home." After she handed me the money, she gave me a hug that seemed to last forever.

I could feel her trembling in my arms and when we separated, I could see she had been crying again. I felt responsible for making her sad.

"I love you, Peter," she said, squeezing me tight.

"I love you, too, Mom." I held my breath for what seemed like a whole minute, trying to keep from crying long enough to say something to her. "What was she like?"

My mother pulled back, holding her hands on my shoulders, keeping her arms straight while blinking back her tears and looking at me. She took a moment before answering, "She was such an angel," Mom said. "We did everything together. She helped me cook and clean and she loved drawing. I saved all her drawings and had them on the walls all over the house."

"What happened to them?" I asked.

"We took them down after she died. It was just too painful to look at them."

I didn't tell my mother, but I made my mind up to find out as much as I could about my sister and how she was killed.

CHAPTER 16
The Fourth of July

~~

S OON JUNE WAS upon us and many kids rejoiced when school let out for the summer. I worked at the pet shop as many days as they allowed, but the majority of my time I could spend with my friends.

When the Fourth of July arrived, the heat was sweltering, causing many in the area to seek an escape from the high temperatures. Rumbles from air conditioning units set on the maximum filled the residential streets of Douglas Creek. Some people didn't have the luxury of air conditioning, so they propped box fans into their open windows, hoping the breeze inside would be sufficient to make life livable during the hottest days of summer.

Tommy and I were invited over to Johnny's house to see the city's fireworks display that night, so we arrived in the afternoon at his house, played, and had supper.

The fireworks usually began when it became dark, which usually meant at about 10 o'clock. Since we still had time to kill, we went outside and rode bicycles until Johnny had an idea.

"Come with me," he said excitedly, running into the garage. He went to a storage rack along the wall of the garage and took a cellophane-wrapped cardboard display box off the shelf. Inside was an assortment of bottle rockets, firecrackers, cherry bombs, black snakes, and a few more assorted fireworks. "Look what my dad bought. He said we can shoot them off after the city fireworks tonight."

"Wow. Let me see," Tommy said with Johnny handing him the box. Tommy looked at everything inside with great interest, while I looked by his side, taking it all in.

"I've shot these off before," Tommy said while putting his index finger on a bottle rocket. "They're cool. They shoot up into the air and go 'bang,' sending sparks everywhere. Let's try one out."

"Right now?" Johnny asked. "No, my dad wouldn't like that. We're supposed to wait until dark."

"He wouldn't miss just one, would he? He wouldn't even notice it was gone," Tommy said while slipping his finger under the cellophane wrap.

"Well, maybe not. But we would need to shoot it off somewhere else," Johnny answered, sounding a little cautious. "Maybe we could take it over to the park or something."

"Yeah, we could do that. What do you think, Peter? Should we do it?" Tommy asked.

I felt a bit frightened but finally nodded.

"Let's go," Tommy said.

Johnny first took two bottle rockets and began to put the package back when he paused for a moment, then removed another bottle rocket before placing the fireworks package on the shelf. He then went to the grill, grabbed the Bic lighter, and the three of us took off down the sidewalk toward the park.

As we got to the park, Tommy slowed his pace and looked blankly ahead, as if deep in thought, then came to a stop.

We stopped, too, and looked inquisitively at Tommy.

"I have a much better idea," he said. "If we shoot them off here while it is still light, we're not going to see much. Let's have a little fun with them instead."

"Like what?" I asked.

"Let's scare someone," Tommy said.

"Like who?" Johnny asked.

A big grin spread across Tommy's face, contemplating what he wanted to do next. "You know how Ralph is always giving you a hard time?"

"Yeah ..." I said cautiously and hesitantly.

"Well, now would be a good time to send him a little message."

"What kind of message? What do you mean?" I wasn't feeling comfortable with the thought of dealing with Ralph at the moment. I thought we were going to have fun.

"I was thinking maybe we could send a few over his house and scare the crap out of him. He lives right over there." Tommy pointed ahead and to his right along the northern edge of the park.

"I don't know. Won't we get into trouble?" I wasn't liking where this was going.

"Yeah, let's do it," Johnny chimed in, eyes wide.

"Come on, Peter. I'm just thinking of shooting them off over his house. The 'boom' will just scare him a little. That's all. Nobody gets hurt."

"I guess so," I said, not wanting to do it, but also not wanting to disappoint Tommy and Johnny. "I just don't want to get caught."

"We won't. Trust me." Tommy took off across the open grassy area to where he had earlier pointed, with Johnny and me not far behind.

When we approached two rows of pine trees, we slowed down. A brown two-story house with white trim stood about 30 feet beyond the trees. Tommy crouched down and used the cover of the trees to get closer. The backyard had a trampoline and a swing set on the grassy area. A barbecue grill and a patio table with an umbrella and chairs sat closer to the house. We laid down on our stomachs to watch and to think about what was to come next.

"Now what?" I asked in a whisper. "I'm not sure we should do this, Tommy. Maybe this is a bad idea."

"No, it's a good idea," Tommy said. "Ralph has been really mean to you and some payback is in order. Besides, a few rockets aren't going to hurt him." We watched the house for movement inside the house through the windows, also waiting for some direction from Tommy. It wasn't long before the back screen door swung open and Ralph's younger sister, Lori, came out. I tensed up at the prospect of being caught. She searched in the grass for a while until she reached down and picked up something.

She swung it around…it was a beaded necklace. "I found it," she yelled as she headed back to the house.

"I told you it was out there," someone yelled, then appeared in a second-story window. It was Ralph. He placed his hands on the bottom of the window ledge to lean out. "You never believe me."

"Mom told you to put the screen back in. You're letting all the bugs in the house," Lori hollered back at him.

"Mind your own business," Ralph told her, then retreated into the house where we couldn't see him anymore.

"Mom!" Lori yelled as she opened the screen door and went inside.

Tommy looked at me and Johnny with a wide grin. "He's here. This ought to be fun." He then looked along the ground around him. "Find a strong stick. We need to dig holes for the ends of the bottle rockets."

We looked around, dismissing several smaller twigs until Johnny found a branch about a half-inch in diameter.

Tommy pushed and wiggled the sharp end of the stick into the ground until he had a hole about two inches deep. He followed that hole with two more, all about a foot apart. Taking each of the rockets, he placed the long stick extending from the bottoms into each of the holes. Examining each from side to side, he gave it a look of dissatisfaction, then took the rockets out and laid them on the ground. "The angle is all wrong," he said like an inventor who wasn't happy with his work. Taking the stick, he jammed it into each of the holes in more of a direction that projected over the house. One of the rockets was a little too angled downward, so he pushed the dirt back into the hole so it sat more upright. Tommy placed the rockets and surveyed his work. "Much better."

"Are you sure about this?" I asked nervously. "I mean, his family is there, too."

"Yeah. Yeah. Let's do this," Johnny said. "This ought to be a blast."

"A blast is right," Tommy said. "Where's the lighter?"

Johnny reached to his back pocket, pulled out the Bic lighter, and handed it to Tommy.

"You ready for this?" Tommy asked. A firm head nod came from Johnny but I didn't answer. A flick of the lever

117

on the lighter and a bright orange-colored flame appeared. "Now get ready to run. As soon as the fuses are lit, we want to get the heck out of here. After those rockets explode, they'll be looking for someone to blame."

Johnny and I weren't waiting for the fuses to be lit. We got up and retreated about 10 feet behind the trees to watch Tommy as he lit the fuses. All eyes were glued to the orange flame. First, one fuse began to glow, then the second and finally the third. Then Tommy got up and ran toward us while we all ran across the grass in the opposite direction. After a few feet, curiosity got the best of us. We stopped to watch.

I wasn't sure if I saw correctly and I wasn't in a position to do anything about it anyway, but I could have sworn I saw the last rocket tilt as Tommy got up to run. It seemed to fall slightly. It was the one in the hole Tommy had to readjust the angle.

The first-lit rocket took off with an *f-s-s-s-t*, faster than could be imagined, towering above the house. About the time the second rocket took off, the first one burst in the air, making a loud "*boom*" and sending a shower of colorful sparks into the sky.

The second took off similarly, bursting about a hundred feet above the house. Someone inside the house screamed, presumably Lori. That's when the third rocket took off. My throat tightened as I saw the rocket take off directly for the side of the house. I froze in horror as we witnessed the ill-fated gag. We saw the rocket take off, destined to crash into the house, but it didn't.

The trajectory was just the perfect recipe for disaster. The rocket disappeared, zipping through the window where Ralph was standing not long ago.

It was like I was paralyzed. My legs couldn't move if they wanted to.

"Yow!" someone screamed from the upstairs bedroom window, in addition to some other louder screams. The rocket made an explosion inside, with a mass of colorful sparks flying about in the room seen through the window. "Aaaaaaah!" came from the window, a cry of extreme distress.

"Let's go!" Johnny yelled to us. Without another word, we ran as fast as we could back towards Johnny's house. I don't think we ever ran that fast before. When we arrived, we went through the open garage door and tried to catch our breaths.

"We are in so much trouble!" I said between gasps. I was bent over, my hands grasping just above my knees. "What are we going to do?"

"Nothing," Tommy said. "No one saw us."

A wail of sirens echoed throughout the city, first coming from the firehouse, then moving through the streets to the direction they had just come from. We knew they were headed to Ralph's house.

"Oh my god," I said, still not breathing normally yet, still bent over. "We are in so much trouble. What if we started their house on fire?"

"Nah, their house isn't on fire. Besides, if it did, the fire department got there right away. Quit worrying about it. As long as no one says anything, nobody will know it was us," Johnny said, putting his hands on my shoulders, apparently trying to calm me down. "We'll be okay."

We tried to do other things in the meantime, trying to occupy ourselves so we wouldn't think about what we had just done and the trouble we may have caused. We played catch with a softball in the backyard until Johnny's mother called us.

"Time to go see the fireworks," she shouted.

"We already saw them," I said under my breath.

Tommy slapped me lightly but firmly with the back of his hand into my stomach. He gave me a look that told me to shut up.

"What?" Johnny's mother frowned, not sure if she heard correctly.

"We can hardly wait," I corrected myself.

Johnny's mom did a double-take, looking at me, but then didn't say anything more about it. "Grab a seat cushion and let's go." She pointed to several colorful stadium seat cushions along the garage wall. The seating in the stands was hard, so cushions made sitting more comfortable.

I was impressed with how organized everything seemed to be, very different from the garage at my home.

Looking over the cushions for our favorite colors or sports teams, we each picked out a cushion and began walking down the sidewalk toward the school ball field.

Johnny's mother and father led the way.

We followed while pushing each other on occasion, punching each other in the arms, and hitting each other with the cushions.

We climbed the steps in the baseball stands and looked for an area where we could all sit together.

Davy Robbins, a kid in my same grade sitting several rows below us, waved to me. He walked up the steps and squeezed in to sit with us. "Hey, did you hear about Ralph? Someone shot fireworks into his house. Everyone is talking about it," Davy said.

I froze, unable to say anything.

"No, we didn't hear. What happened?" Johnny chimed in to answer.

"Ralph is angry he says he's going to find out who did it, I heard," Davy said.

"So, what happened?" Johnny asked.

"He said fireworks flew in his window, almost hit him, bounced off the walls a few times, and then exploded!"

"Wow. Was anyone hurt?" I asked, pretending to not know anything about it.

"No. just left some black marks everywhere supposedly. Ralph is pissed off. He swears he's going to find out and then *POW*, he's going to get him."

Tommy and Johnny cracked a smile, but I did not smile.

We talked a little more about the incident before the fireworks began, but then a large *boom* marked the beginning of the fireworks show. Davy went back to his seat.

After the fireworks finished, we went back to Johnny's house and his father got out the package of fireworks from the garage. He looked carefully at the opened cellophane and then eyed Johnny. "What happened here?" he asked.

"I don't know," Johnny answered, avoiding looking directly at his father.

"Yeah, I'm sure," his father said.

We set up some lawn chairs on the driveway and shot off the remaining fireworks one-by-one, then agreed it was time to go home.

Johnny's mother drove each of us to our houses.

When I got into the safety of my bedroom and locked the door, I sat on the edge of my bed. I told Chockie everything that happened.

"So, how do you feel about it? Are you happy or do you feel bad for what happened to Ralph? Or are you more afraid?" Chockie asked.

"Now you are sounding like my counselor at school," I said.

"Really? You think I could get a job as a counselor?" Chockie joked.

"Yeah. In your dreams," I said in amusement.

"Actually, in my dreams, I've done a lot of things," Chockie said. "Back to the subject at hand. What are you thinking?"

"Well, I'm a little sorry about what happened. I mean, the rocket flying into his house wasn't intentional, but it does seem rather mean. I wish we hadn't done it." I stared at the floor, thinking about the moment the fireworks took off and flew into the open window. I let out a little chuckle. "But it was kind of funny, too."

"Yeah, it sure seems funny to me. A little dangerous though, huh?" Chockie asked.

"I suppose. Ralph could have been hurt. Maybe even the house could have burned down," I said, feeling a little ashamed.

"So, it wasn't so much fun being the bully?"

"No, not really. I mean, I kind of wanted to get back at Ralph for all the mean things he's done to me, but now that I had the chance, it doesn't make me as happy as I thought it would," I said.

"Lesson learned," Chockie said.

I looked at Chockie with amazement. It seemed like Chockie knew how I felt about it. It seemed like Chockie was the wise guru on top of the mountain who had been contemplating the meaning of life for years. "Dang Chockie. You are too smart for me." I said.

"Well, you know what they say: Fish is brain food," Chockie said. "Food for thought, anyway."

CHAPTER 17

Camping Trip

A FRIEND AND CLASSMATE of mine, Alex Simmons, was having a birthday, so he wanted to celebrate it with me and some other friends by going camping.

So, Alex's father asked my mom if I could go with Alex and a bunch of our friends. His father agreed to take us. We were to have Alex's birthday party at a campground up North.

I felt excited to go. I'd never been camping before and I thought it would be great to spend a summer night in the outdoors. I always dreamed of a camping trip, but my father wasn't in favor of the idea so my family never made a venture into the woods for a night.

Five boys were invited for his birthday camping trip, including Tommy, Johnny, Zack, Drew, and me, all friends in the eighth grade at Douglas Creek Junior High School.

Alex's dad packed up all the tents then offered sleeping bags and mattresses to anyone not bringing his own.

We headed to the north woods of Wisconsin, an area filled with many lakes. Our destination was Lake Owen, a long slender glacier lake that extended for 10 miles with crystal clear water, or so Alex's dad told us.

When we arrived at a campground along the banks of Lake Owen a little past noon, all of us piled out of the minivan and ran directly to the water's edge. We breathed in the fresh cooler air, filled with pine tree scents from all the pine trees around us, along with the smells of the freshwater lake.

Since we hadn't eaten lunch yet, Alex's dad brought out a bag of charcoal and poured some briquettes into the grill mounted on a pipe cemented to the ground. After dousing the charcoal with lighter fluid, Mr. Blume lit the coals with towering flames. He waited about a minute for the flames to die down before placing about a dozen hot dogs on the grill.

We skipped stones across the lake surface and walked down the shoreline before gathering to eat and then set up tents. Tommy and I made sure to share a tent, while Johnny and Zack shared one then Drew and Alex shared another. Alex's dad had a tent of his own.

That afternoon, we took turns taking out the canoe on the lake, with Alex's father making sure we all wore our life vests. We enjoyed paddling on the lake but we were given instructions not to travel too far away from camp.

I could hardly contain my excitement. My mind started swirling on how I could get my mother and father to take me camping, so the whole family could experience it.

That evening, Alex's father threw some chicken on the grill then provided potato chips and pop. We horsed around for a while before pulling up some chairs around the campfire to tell some stories. The atmosphere was spooky with loons on the lake. The eerie, haunting, and beautiful sounds made by this bird … the loon. Loons make a sound that is very distinctive and unique.

Alex's dad piled the firewood so the air swirled beneath the flames and sent embers towering into the night air. An occasional pop would emanate from the wood, sending embers flying a short distance upward with the sudden sound, causing us to flinch at first.

The darkness encircled us, causing our world to grow a little smaller into the tiny circle of lightness with the outside world a mystery. An occasional howl from a distant wolf would cause us to sit upright and perk our ears to the secrets of the nighttime wildlife. Several hoots from owls in various spots encircling our camp caused us to tilt our heads back and look up into the trees, although the darkness would not reveal its treasure. Light smiles broke out onto our faces, giving credence that we were truly enjoying the moment.

"Okay, who has a story to tell?" Alex's father asked, looking into our shadowy fire-lit faces.

We were silent, looking at each other and afraid to speak up first.

Finally, one of us broke the silence, "You have a lot of stories, Dad. Why don't you tell one of them?" Alex asked.

"Okay, I guess I can, seeing that none of you have any," he said. "Once there was a bear hunter who was hunting in these very woods. He had been walking all day, searching for a big bear the locals called Wilbur. The bear was as big as they get and anyone who had ever seen him was terrified. The rumor was that he got his name because a local man, Wilbur Jenkins, disappeared about the time the bear made his appearance. Many people believed that the bear ate Wilbur, so everyone just called the bear Wilbur. The hunter, whose name was Andrew, was heading back to his car because it was getting dark and he hadn't seen anything all day. He had just walked through a stand of pines when he came around a big rock and came face-to-face with Wilbur, standing on his hind legs and growling." Alex's father put both hands up into a claw-like grip and bore his teeth as much as possible. "Andrew looked up to see the bear's face, his teeth big and long, ready to chomp down on him. The hunter was so scared, he dropped his rifle and couldn't move. 'Don't eat me,' the hunter cried out to the bear. Surprisingly, the bear stopped growling and got down on all four feet, but still kept his eyes on the hunter.'

We were nearly holding our breaths as Alex's dad paused.

" 'I won't eat you,' the bear said to the surprise of the hunter, 'but you have to promise not to ever shoot me. I have been living in these woods for 10 years and I always have to hide from humans because they all want to shoot me.' The man could hardly comprehend the bear talking to him, but finally, he relaxed and realized he was no longer in danger. 'Okay. I won't shoot you. But I can't promise someone else won't try to harm you. You're a legend in these woods.'

" 'If there was only a way that people would leave me alone. I mean no harm to anyone,' the bear said. The hunter sympathized with the bear and tried to think of a way the bear could live in the woods and not be shot. Then he got an idea. He told the bear he would buy him clothes so that anyone seeing him would think he was a human. The hunter went into town and bought the largest jacket and pants he could find, came back, and gave them to the bear. He even helped the bear put them on. The legend to this day is that Wilbur roams these woods and looks just like a human being. So, the next time you see someone walking around the woods in hunting clothes, take a close look to see if it is a person or Wilbur in disguise. Oh, and one more thing. Wilbur loves to visit campers at night to see if one of them is Andrew so he can thank him. So, if you hear growling outside your tent tonight, it might be Wilbur."

Some of us made an "ooo-ing" sound. I'm not sure if we were scared or just pretending to be.

"I have one," Drew said. "My grandpa used to tell a story every time we went camping about this thing called the Hillcrawler. It was a human creature thing that had one normal-sized leg and then one super long, crooked leg so it could walk around the edges of steep hills with no struggle - almost in a splits-like position. I didn't think much of it at the time but now, that I'm out here, it kind of scares the heck out of me."

"Creepy!" Zack said.

We sat in silence for a few moments, staring at the fire while it crackled.

Johnny grabbed a stick and poked into the fire.

"Hey Tommy, you have a scary story, don't you?" I asked.

"What story?"

"You know – the story of the goatman," I replied.

"It's not a camping story. It's part of Ho-Chunk culture. It's true," Tommy said.

"What is it?" Drew asked.

"Yeah, tell us," Alex encouraged.

"Well, okay, I'm not sure I'm supposed to be telling you guys this, but in Ho-Chunk beliefs, there is a goatman who lives around us but is seldom seen. He's half goat and half man. I know of several people who have seen it," Tommy said. "People have seen it at night, usually. What I am told is that if you can catch the goatman and hold onto him until sunrise, he has to answer all your questions."

All of us were glued to Tommy's every word. We waited

for more but we soon realized Tommy wasn't going to say anything more.

"What do you mean? What questions does the goatman answer?" I asked.

"Any questions. Anything you want to ask him. He has to answer everything truthfully," Tommy said.

"Cool!" Johnny said. "I'd like to find that goatman. I'd ask him what the winning lottery numbers are."

"I thought you would have asked if Jennifer Hanson loves you," Drew teased.

Johnny's face turned red and the boys started laughing. He got up and angrily pushed Drew in the chest.

"Now, now, boys!" Alex's father interceded. "Let's take it easy. No more teasing. Johnny, take your seat."

Johnny returned to his chair, obviously still embarrassed by Drew's comment.

Many of us talked about the possibility of having any questions answered, talking about what they would ask the goatman.

Everyone was discussing the idea before Alex's dad finally broke the murmuring.

"Anyone else has a story to tell?"

A few seconds passed before Zack spoke up. "I have one." Zack cleared his throat before beginning while collecting his thoughts. "My uncle Joe was driving home late one night when he picked up a pretty girl in a white dress while she was hitchhiking. The girl was very nice and they have a good conversation. He finds out her name is Beth. He drove her home and dropped Beth off at her house. The next day, he got in his car and found that she left her sweater on the seat. He decided to drive over and drop the sweater off at her house. Besides, he wanted to see her again."

A couple of us made the sound "oooo," like we were teasing him about his uncle wanting to see the girl.

"When he rang the bell," Zack continued, "an old lady answered the door. My uncle tells her the story of him giving Beth a ride and the old lady tells him he must be mistaken – her daughter Beth died in a car accident after a night of dancing 20 years ago."

"Wow," many of us said, with some of us looking at each other in surprise.

No more scary stories were told, but we spent some time roasting marshmallows on the end of pointed sticks and some were making s'mores.

Several of us yawned, which gave Alex's dad a signal to call it a night. "Okay, boys, time to hit the tents," he said. "You'll want to brush your teeth and go to the bathroom first." He handed out some flashlights for us to go to the outdoor latrines.

We paired up to sleep in our tents, while Alex's dad crawled into his tent. The tents were illuminated with battery-powered lanterns or flashlights and we were too excited to attempt sleep yet.

"So, is that goatman real?" I asked anxiously.

"As far as I know. I mean, I've never actually seen it, but there are plenty of people who have told me they did. Stories of the goatmen have been around for generations."

"You said if you catch one, it will answer any question? So, these goatmen have all the answers?"

"That's what I have been told. Why? What question would you ask?" Tommy must have seen that I was very curious about it.

"Well, I have a couple of questions. Are you allowed more than one question?"

"Yes. All the questions you can ask."

"Well, I want to know more about my dad. Most of the time he's quite distant – even when he's right there," I said. "And Ralph – why does he pick on me and what I can do to get him to stop." I stared into the lantern. "Also, I would like to ask about Chockie. How can a fish talk? How is that possible?"

"Wow. Those are some good questions, Peter. I'm thinking we need to find that goatman," Tommy said. "When we get back home, I'll ask around more about him."

I wasn't sure if he was serious or just joking with me.

Tommy laid back in his sleeping bag and turned off the lantern. "Good night."

I remained sitting up, my legs inside the sleeping bag. I didn't answer right away. I was still deep in thought.

After a few minutes, I laid back and zipped up my sleeping bag.

"Good night, Tommy," I said.

CHAPTER 18
Peter Digs More Into The Past

~‿᳁

I WAS SAD TO see summer come to an end. The worst part of the summer ending was the start of school when all my free time turned into doing schoolwork. It also was scary because this was my first year of high school. I was a freshman.

Football games began and the warmer days soon became a memory.

Rain poured from the skies, the trees shed their leaves and a cold wind cut me to the bone as autumn set in… winter was knocking on the door. Many of my outdoor activities seemed to cease and I retreated to the inside comfort of my home during the series of blustery days.

Chockie became a steady source of amusement for me, as I often spent my time at Chockie's side, doing my homework, listening to music, and playing games on my Xbox.

Chockie thrived in his new tank, growing even bigger

and becoming an expert in conversation. He seemed to delve into more philosophical debates, while I tried to steer him more into my world, telling him about what it's like to live outside the aquarium. Chockie often wondered what it would be like to live in the big waters, in the wild, since he had been born and raised in captivity. He knew the stories of the wild but never lived there.

Chockie knew a lot about aquatic life despite having been separated from the rest of his family at an early age. Some of his knowledge was innate, having been born with the instinct, other knowledge he had acquired from his parents after he was born, some from his siblings, and still other knowledge that I suspected he had just made up.

Some statements just seemed to be too outlandish to be true, I sometimes thought.

I told Chockie that I had been avoiding any contact with Ralph and his buddies, often taking different and exhausting routes from school to the pet shop. I avoided talking about the subject with anyone but Chockie.

"We have bullies in the water, too," Chockie told me. "We can either fight back or swim away. It's our choice and there's no shame in swimming."

I reasoned that when Chockie was young, he must have lived in a school with his siblings, so he probably did experience some aggression. However, I doubted Chockie could relate to what happens on dry land.

I had a television in my room and I moved it so Chockie could see better. I often played DVDs with underwater scenes. Chockie didn't like movies like Jaws, but he did like the old Flipper television series, plus anything with Jacques Cousteau.

One Saturday afternoon, I was playing some video games on my Xbox when I grew tired of it and laid on my bed for a few minutes. I turned to Chockie, who was spitting out some gravel from his mouth. He often liked to rearrange his surroundings.

"I wonder what my sister was like. I think about her often, even though I don't remember ever meeting her," I said.

"You mean Sarah?"

"Yeah. Sarah. It would have been nice to have an older sister. I hinted to Mom that I'd like to know more about her but she won't, or can't, talk about it."

"She can't talk about her?"

"No, she gets choked up and crying and she feels bad and I feel bad for her, so we never get to talk about her."

"Ask your father."

"Yeah, right," I said sarcastically. "I can't talk to him about anything. You know that. He can be fun sometimes, but I always have to be prepared for him to explode."

"Explode? Like fly apart and go '*boom*'?"

"No, that means for him to suddenly change his mood. Sometimes he yells and even throws things without hardly any warning. Anything can set him off. He scares me sometimes."

"Have you ever told him that?"

"I can't. I can't even tell him anything about what's going on in my life. It's like he's a stranger most of the time, although I do love him. He is my dad."

"You need to tell him that.

"Yeah," I said, looking down at the floor. "Yeah. Maybe I do."

The whole subject made me uncomfortable. I didn't feel like talking anymore, so I returned to playing games, but I soon lost interest. I threw the controller on the bed, walked out of my room, and headed for the garage. I was home alone, so I wanted to check out something before my parents got home. Once inside the garage, I looked over all the plastic storage totes that were stacked in two rows in the corner. I looked up and down, searching for that certain blue one.

"Aha," I said, then got out the stepladder and began disassembling the stack until the blue tote I was looking for was on the garage floor. Unsnapping the lid, I saw the framed picture wrapped in the white paper – the same picture I had discovered earlier. Digging into the tub, I carefully took out each item and placed them nearby on the floor. I found many more photos of Sarah and many school papers, including her artwork. Along the side of the tub was a large manila envelope with the top flap clasped.

Bending the metal clasps outward, I flipped open the top of the envelope and peered inside. It was a newspaper clipping, so I carefully slid it out so I could examine it more closely.

It was a front-page story from the Yorktown Examiner, the daily paper from the nearest large city, dated July 6, 2006. It had a horrific picture of a twisted car and the headline read, "*Two children die in head-on crash.*" This sent shock waves through me, knowing that my sister must have been one of them, but I wanted to know who was the other person, and how did the crash occur.

My mind raced as my eyes scanned the words as quickly as possible.

Two 12-year old girls were killed in an accident involving an SUV and a semi-truck Tuesday night at the intersection of Highway 53 and Springfield Drive, north of Douglas Creek. Spruce County Coroner Rick Sheffield pronounced the girls, Sarah Brighton and Brenda Higgins, dead at the scene. Injured and transported to

Yorktown Memorial Hospital was James D. Brighton, the driver of the SUV. He has been listed in serious condition. The driver of the other vehicle, Theodore P. Caldwell, received minor injuries and is listed in good condition at Yorktown Memorial Hospital," the article said. *Spruce County Sheriff Roger Drake said a toxicology report has been ordered and alcohol could not be ruled out as a contributing factor.*

I stopped reading at that point, putting the article back into the manila envelope and placing it on the workbench. I piled all the items back into the plastic tote and snapped on the lid. The tote went back onto the pile and the other totes were stacked neatly on top as they had been.

I checked the floor and surrounding area to make sure I didn't forget anything. Everything looked the same as it had before. Satisfied, I grabbed the envelope and headed for my bedroom.

My mind was reeling. My father was the driver and he was possibly drunk at the time. Who was the other girl, Brenda Higgins, and what was she doing in the car?

I could hardly wait to read the rest of the article, taking the envelope into my room and shutting the door. I was about to take out the newspaper clipping when I heard the garage door opening.

Either it was my mother or my father, but either way, I didn't want to get caught with the article. I slipped it under the mattress on my bed.

Heading out my bedroom door and down the hallway, I watched as the door from the garage into the house slowly opened. It was my mother carrying two brown paper grocery bags, one in each arm pulled tightly to her chest so she wouldn't drop them. "Peter," my mom called out. "Help me carry in the groceries."

I quickly approached her and took the bags from her,

placing them on the kitchen island, and then went out to the car for more. When I retrieved all the groceries from the car, I helped my mother place the food in the cupboards, pantry, and refrigerator. All the while doing so, I was building up the courage to ask her a question. "Mom," I said hesitantly, "can I ask you a question?"

"You already did," she answered, then snickered. "Just kidding. What is it?"

"I was just wondering," I stopped for a moment, thinking over my words. "Why didn't you ever tell me that I had a sister? Why did you keep it from me? Why didn't you ever tell me that she died?" I became more worked up the more I talked.

"It wasn't easy, Peter." She came over to hug me. "It wasn't my idea. Your father never wanted me to tell you. We were not supposed to talk about it. It upsets him very much. Oh, Peter, I wanted to – believe me. It has been eating inside me for so long." Tears were freely flowing down her cheeks. "You don't know how this has torn me up. I wanted to die so many times, but the only thing that kept me going is you. You needed me at that time and that is what held me together. You needed me and I needed you even more," she said, giving me a strong, long hug.

"What happened? I mean, I know it was a car crash, but what was it all about?"

"Oh, God…" My mother took a moment and swallowed hard before answering. "Your father was taking Brenda home, Sarah's friend. She had been over to our house for the afternoon. Your father had been drinking and I had taken you to the store with me to get diapers. Well, he ran a stop sign and was hit by a semi-truck. It was bad. Ever since then, your father does not want to talk about it. Sometimes, I think he blames me, but most of the time he's angry with himself. I know he doesn't treat you right, either. Your father is a changed man. He is different now than he was before the accident."

"I was wondering what I did wrong so that he hates me so much," I said.

"I know your dad doesn't always communicate with you well, but he is a good man. He's got a good heart and he loves you very much. He keeps a lot of his emotions inside himself. That's why he likes to spend time in the garage, working on cars. He likes his alone time to fight with his demons. He just doesn't know how to express his feelings."

I looked into my mother's eyes, full of tears, and felt my mother's sorrow through her arms as she held me tight. "I'm so sorry, Mom."

"I know, honey. I know," she said, pulling me even tighter to her body.

"There's just one more question," I looked into my mother's eyes as she released her grip. "Sarah's friend – Brenda. Her last name was Higgins. Ralph's last name is Higgins."

His mother took a deep breath. "Yes, they were related. Brenda was Ralph's sister."

I had a sinking feeling. I was at a loss for words and many thoughts ran through my mind. "Do you suppose …" I asked, "that's why—"

"I think so," she said, pulling me back into a hug. "I really think so."

CHAPTER 19
Problems Seem Small

~~~~~~2

HE NEXT TIME I was alone in the house, I went into the kitchen and retrieved the step-stool my mother always used for reaching some things on the cabinet top shelves. Taking it to the spare bedroom, I opened the closet door and placed it where I could reach some of the top shelves above the clothes rack. The boxes always intrigued me, but I always dismissed them as a place where my mother stored extra clothing, or maybe some dishes and other household things.

Something had been stirring in me since I found out about my sister. I wanted to know more, but I quickly found it wasn't as easy as asking my mother or father. My mother obviously was carrying around a lot of pent-up feelings about Sarah and her death, so she had a difficult time talking about it. From what I could tell, her ability to talk about it wasn't being helped by my father's anger and control over the issue. Talking about it with my father wasn't even a consideration.

I knew about the extra bedroom and that it had a bed in

it, but it was a very rare occasion anyone would sleep in it. Once in a great while, a relative from a long-distance came to visit and slept in the bed, but it didn't happen that often. I noticed the walls were painted pink, hardly a color the average person would choose to paint the walls of a room unless there was a girl involved. It had never dawned on me until now.

Now was my chance to investigate the mystery a little further, since my father was at work and my mother was cleaning someone's house, as she did several times a week.

I climbed up the steps and took a top box from a stack on the left. Bringing it down onto the floor, I lifted the box lid and peered within. Inside were more memories: photos, stuffed animals, papers and artwork from school, and a little jewelry box. It was apparent to me that my mother was hiding Sarah's possessions. I understood that throwing these away made her feel as though she was letting her go and even like a betrayal of her memory.

My eyes immediately caught the little jewelry box situated along the side and nearly at the bottom, so I reached deep into the box and pulled it out. It was a soft, fuzzy box, a little larger than a box made for a ring. I held the box in my hand and stared at it for a moment, understanding that this may have been very important to my sister. I grasped the top and swung it back, revealing a gold heart inside, attached to a delicate gold chain necklace. The gold heart was domed and sitting halfway into the cardboard cutout.

I gently took it out from the box, placing it in the center of my palm while standing at the entrance of the closet. I could see it had a crease that separated the front half from the back and a tab on that split. Pressing against the tab, the cover flipped open so fast it startled me. I had never seen anything like it.

My eyes were instantly glued to what was inside the two halves of the locket. Pressed inside were two pictures. On the left half, I could see it was my father and mother, very young, probably soon after they were married. In the other half was a picture of a baby, maybe a year old. I studied both pictures closely, but mostly the baby picture. Somehow, I knew the picture was of me. At first, I felt glad to see my sister thought enough of me to carry my photo around her neck, and everywhere she went. But then I felt enormous sorrow and of great loss that someone who loved me, and she was someone I could have loved so much, was gone. I would never see her. I stared intensely, trying to find the fragments in my memory that told me who she was when I was a baby.

My thoughts and emotions were changing so rapidly and my eyes were darting between the two photos that I didn't hear my mother enter the house and approach the doorway to the bedroom.

"Peter?" my mother asked softly. She caught me staring at the locket in my hand. She first had the look of wonder, but then she had the look of recognition of what was in my hand.

My trance was broken when I heard her voice. Surprisingly, I wasn't jolted by her sudden appearance. I said nothing, looked at her, then looked back at the locket.

My mother came to my side, placed her arm around my shoulders, and looked at the locket.

I turned my body and wrapped my arms around her, bursting into tears.

When my sobbing subsided enough for me to get a few words out, I asked, "Why? Why did she have to die? I didn't even get to know her."

"I know, Peter," my mother said, resting her cheek

against the top of my head while pulling me tightly to her. "I know. It isn't fair. None of any of it is fair. Not fair to you, not fair to us and certainly not fair to Sarah."

I sniffed back my tears, let go of my tight grip, and sat on the edge of the bed while holding my hand down by my lap to look again at the locket.

"What was she like?" It was a simple question, obviously not one with a simple answer, but I was so captivated by the thought of Sarah that I wanted to know every detail in an attempt to form an image in my mind of how she might have looked and behaved. I just wanted to fill the hole of emptiness I felt. Sometimes, I could feel her presence, but perhaps it was nothing more than memories of her from when I was very young.

"I think it's time I took you with me," my mother said.

"What? Took me where?" I frowned, confused about what she was talking about.

"Just trust me," she said. "I should have done this, years ago."

We went out into the garage and climbed into my mother's 1998 Buick Le Sabre… an old clunker with nearly 300,000 miles on it and it always needed repair, but Dad was always tinkering with it to keep it going.

My mother drove down Main Street with me still wondering where we were going. When she pulled into a flower shop along the way, I thought we had arrived at our destination and I began getting out of the car.

"Just wait here. I'll only be a couple of minutes," she said and left the car with the motor running.

I could hear the bells at the top of the flower shop door tinkled as she walked in without hesitation. It was as if she had done this before.

She returned within a couple of minutes, just like she said, carrying an assortment of flowers, in all colors, in some brown wrapping paper. Placing it loosely in the backseat, she got back in the driver's seat, shut the door, and took off.

"What are the flowers for?"

"You'll see in a couple of minutes. Just sit tight."

The car rolled down a few side streets until we came upon a huge gate with concrete pillars on either side, iron fencing extending to both sides of the pillars.

The turn was sharp, but she managed to pull into the drive like she could have done it in her sleep.

I looked about and saw that we had just entered the city cemetery. Headstones extended in rows as far as I could see.

Going to the back edge of the cemetery, my mother came to a stop, shut off the engine, and got out of the car. "Come on," she said.

I followed her from the car, walking between the headstones. I noticed that some were decorated with flowers and some with small United States flags, but most headstones had nothing.

My mother came to a stop in front of a headstone that was surrounded by many flowers, some ceramic dolls, and a teddy bear. The display stood out from all the other graves which, compared to Sarah's, looked plain and lonely.

The headstone read:

Sarah Brighton

May 12, 1994 – July 6, 2006

Our little miracle is now God's angel

My mother placed the flowers with the rest, taking some of the wilted ones away.

"Who put all these flowers and stuff here?" I asked.

"I did," my mother said. "I come here almost every chance I get, weather permitting, of course."

"Does Dad come here, too?"

"Sometimes," she said faintly. "Well, he's busy, you know, with work. I usually come here during the weekday when he's not able to."

"I see." I decided not to press the issue and resumed looking at the headstone while trying to imagine how my mother must feel.

My mother clasped her hands, bowed her head, and held her eyes shut.

I figured that she must be praying, so I stood quietly and waited for her to finish. I didn't know what else to do.

When she finished, she looked up at me.

"Mom?"

"Yes?" she asked.

"I can't imagine what that was like, you know, having her die and everything," I said. I imagined seeing her in an open coffin; looking rather pale and having someone apply some type of makeup to make her look alive. I'd seen that at a funeral with my parents, but I'd been too afraid to get close to the coffin. The person looked so plastic and unreal. The vision still haunted me and I feared to go anywhere near a dead body. After this, I had a fear of death and I would rather avoid any part of it.

I put my arms around her waist from the side and laid my head against her.

She laid her hand on my head to comfort me. "Yes, it was difficult. It still is. She is in heaven now and everything is much better up there."

I fell silent for a while, thinking about it. I wondered what heaven was all about and where it existed. Everyone says heaven is up, but do they mean in the clouds, in space, in the center of the universe, or where? And the even more confusing part was that we end up in heaven forever. I can't imagine forever. "This makes our little problems seem pretty small, doesn't it?" I asked. "I mean, all the stuff we go through every day – it doesn't mean much. Our lives together are more important. Our family is more important."

All the problems I thought about day after day – the bullying, how I hated school, and all the things that went with it – all seemed to melt away. It wasn't so important anymore.

My mother smiled when she heard this, holding me close to her side. She stared up at the clouds. "You're right, Peter. When someone you love dies, it puts everything into perspective. Love is much more important."

CHAPTER 20
Science Fair

I LOOKED AT MY notebook blankly while sitting on my bed, and then tossed the notebook down beside me.

"What's wrong? Do you have some difficult homework?" Chockie asked, swimming back and forth as if he were pacing.

"Yeah, I guess you could say that," I said sadly. "We have this science fair coming up and I have to come up with a project that I can put on display. I don't want to do the volcano thing that everyone else is doing. I want to do something different – something exciting and ... well, just different."

"That is a difficult one," Chockie said, stopping at the center of the glass. "You could show them your video games skills."

"Na," I said. "Everyone plays video games. I want to do something with nature. Plants or wildlife or something."

"Why don't you show them a tree? Maybe describe the

different kinds of trees and show their leaves. I like the leaves. I grab bugs off of them."

"Yeah, I suppose I could do that," I said while deep in thought. I wasn't too excited about the tree suggestion and was still searching for ideas. Suddenly, a thought came to me and I sat upright. "I could show you!"

"Wait a minute here. Me? No, no, no. I'm not liking the sound of that."

"Oh, come on. It'll be fun. I could see if I could borrow a tank from Mitch and set it up in the gym—"

"What? I'm not liking this too much. What would happen then? Everyone would come and stare at me, and pound on the glass as they did at the pet shop. People are insane, especially little kids. They knock on the glass as if I'm going to do tricks for them or something. You don't know what those shock waves do to my nervous system."

"Do tricks? Hey, yeah. That's a great idea."

"Oh, my god. Peter, are you even listening to me?"

"I could set up a series of rings that you could swim through at my command."

"What? Do I look like Shamu at Sea World? Let's get real here. I am not the performing type. I am your everyday, garden-variety chocolate cichlid. I cannot do tricks. It's not even in my contract … if I had a contract."

"Yeah," I said, staring into space, not even listening to what Chockie said. I grabbed my notebook and began sketching out a scene.

"Now let's talk about this. We need to keep our heads straight on this," Chockie pleaded. "I'm not comfortable around other people, you know."

"Don't worry," I said, not even looking up from my paper, "I've got everything under control."

"That's what I'm afraid of."

I spent the next three weeks making the training equipment to fit into the aquarium and then teaching Chockie how to use it. I kept Mitch informed about the project and its progress, so when the date of the science fair arrived, everyone was ready to go.

On the day of the science fair, masking tape was placed on the gymnasium floor to section off the assigned areas, with the names of the students written on the tape. Mitch helped me move a heavy stand into the gymnasium and to my designated place. It was a stand with an oak exterior and doors below. Behind the doors were two shelves intended to hold fish food and other equipment. Mitch carried in an empty 30-gallon tank and placed it squarely on top of the stand.

I had previously siphoned water from Chockie's tank at home into a few five-gallon plastic pails. The same water was being used so as not to cause shock to Chockie, plus the school's water was city water, which had chlorine in it. Mitch and I agreed that the science fair was only for one day and we didn't want to shock Chockie. Otherwise, we would have to condition the water, and even then, with new water chemistry, it might be bad for him. It wasn't worth the chance just for a few hours of the science fair, so we brought our own water.

Mitch lifted the pails high and poured the water into the tank while I got a power filter and a 100-watt aquarium heater going, connecting to a power cord that was taped firmly to the floor. When the setup was running well for about 20 minutes, Mitch stood with his hands on his hips, looking at the tank and then at me.

"I want to thank you for helping me," I said. "I never could have done this alone."

"No problem, dude," Mitch said. "We're a well-oiled machine. This stuff is heavy and I wouldn't want you breaking your back over this. Besides, this looks rather fun. I want to see the reactions of your classmates when they see Chockie do all those amazing acts." He stepped over to the tank and placed his index finger in the water to gauge the temperature. "What do you think? Are you ready? Is Chockie ready?"

"Yeah, I think so. I don't think he's too happy in that bucket," I answered while staring into the pail below. "Should we use the towel to transfer him or pour him in with the water?"

"It probably would be less stress if we could gently pour him into the tank."

I agreed.

Mitch lifted the pail high above the aquarium and began pouring the water, with Chockie staying at the bottom. When half the water in the pail was gone, Mitch tipped the pail horizontal, with the side of the pail entering the aquarium water. Chockie took that opportunity to swim forward and plunge into the tank. Mitch then lifted the pail out.

I breathed a sigh of relief. The transfer seemed easy and Chockie was just fine, swimming and looking around his new environment.

Mitch stuffed much of the fish support items on the shelves in the stand, including a small container of mealworms, and then grabbed the empty buckets to take them to his car. When Mitch was out the door, I looked around to make sure no one was in the gym except me and Chockie. "How are you doing, Chockie? I know it might be scary, but I'll be right here," I whispered.

"I told you I don't like this. That bucket experience was

the worst. I could hardly turn around in that little space. Tell me I don't have to do that again," Chockie said softly.

"Well, there is the trip home, but let's not worry about that right now. Listen up because I don't have much time to talk. I'm going to set up the rings in this tank and when I tell you, you need to do just like we practiced at home. Please? My grade depends on it," I pleaded.

"If it means getting this over with and me getting back home sooner, then yeah. Let's get this over with."

Mitch returned when I had my arms in the water, sticking the large colored plastic rings with suction cups to the inside glass of the aquarium. I placed a small black box to the end of the tank.

"Ready?" Mitch asked.

I nodded. "Let's try it." I pushed a button on the black box and one of the rings lit up. Chockie promptly swam through it.

"Good going, Chockie!" I said, then reached into a box and retrieved a treat, dropping it into the water for Chockie to eat. "I think we're ready."

I repeated the trick, this time lighting a different ring, with Chockie swimming through the proper ring. A mealworm was his treat for doing it correctly.

Bells rang throughout the school and classroom doors flew open. The noise of children came from everywhere and many of them began to file into the gymnasium, each going to their displays and preparing for the upcoming show.

Chockie began to get nervous, looking at all the motion around him and began to dash about the tank in a frenzy. Water splashed out the open top of the aquarium and onto the floor. I quickly grabbed one of the towels and placed it over the entire aquarium, then took another towel to soak up the mess. "Calm down, Chockie. It's okay. I'm right here and no one's going to harm you," I said in a soothing voice while peeking beneath the towel.

"I think the sudden motion scared him," Mitch said. "In nature, when fish see fast movement, it usually means they are under attack from some predator. It's probably best to leave the towel on the tank until everything is set and we're ready for the show. It will keep him calm."

Mitch and I made sure everything was in order, then watched as the other students worked on their science displays. Some students had projects of green energy, such as solar power, wind power, and even a potato-powered clock and light bulb. Still, others had displays of recycled materials and the products they could create from them. And of course, there were a couple of volcanoes, something I always saw at science fairs. After scanning the crowd, I was confident I had the best and most unique project.

"You have five more minutes to get ready," Mrs. Richardson shouted across the gym. Her voice was so loud, the constant din of voices came to an abrupt halt. "Students from other classes will be entering soon and they'll be grading your displays, so give them a good explanation of your project. This will go on for 30 minutes. Once they leave, you'll have plenty of time to take down your displays." Mrs. Richardson walked over to a table at one of the gym entrances and began to get the evaluation forms in order.

Talking began again across the gym and became a deafening roar. I took another look beneath the towel.

Chockie looked flushed with a light color indicating he was stressed and trying to hide in a corner.

"Okay, Chockie, l whispered. "You only have to do this a few times, just like we rehearsed. You can do this. I need to get a good grade on this and it all depends on you. I know you're nervous, but just concentrate on doing your act."

Chockie just looked at me and didn't move.

"Come on, Chockie. Relax. It'll all be over soon." I removed my head from beneath the towel.

A couple more minutes passed before students lined up behind the table just inside the gym entrance. Each was given a clipboard, a grading sheet, a pen, and instructions on how to grade each display. As they departed the table, they spread out among the displays to begin their evaluations.

"Okay, you're on," Mitch said. "I'll watch you from the back of the gym. You got this." He walked away.

A large group formed in front of my demonstration, which I couldn't quite understand. I looked around me and saw more students in front of my project than any other. "My project is concerning animal behavior and how animals, including fish, can learn from humans through positive reinforcement," I said to the dozen children standing before me, my nervous voice wavering a little. I slowly drew back the towel to show Chockie cowering in a corner of the aquarium.

The kids shuffled about, trying to get a better look.

"This is Chockie. He is a chocolate cichlid and comes from the Amazon River basin in South America. I will demonstrate how he will do particular tasks for rewards, considered conditional training." I pushed a button and the end ring lighted.

Chockie didn't move, staying in the corner, head down.

My face must have turned red because I felt flushed from embarrassment. I tried lighting another ring. Chockie didn't move.

The students began to talk among themselves, a kind of buzz that indicated that they were disappointed. I turned my back to the group and squatted down to Chockie's level. "Come on, Chockie, you can do it," I pleaded.

Someone in the group came forward to stand at the front. I turned to see it was Ralph.

"What's the matter? Is your fish dead?" Ralph asked. "He looks big enough to eat. Why don't I take him home with me and eat him tonight for supper?" Some of the students behind him laughed. Ralph pounded on the glass with the heel of his fist. "Come on, fishy. Move!"

Anger welled up in me. I didn't like being picked on, but making insults and threats to Chockie was more than I could take. I grabbed Ralph's right arm and gave him a shove. "Knock it off, Ralph!" I shouted. I could tell that Ralph was surprised I'd pushed him. I figured that, by yelling, I drew the attention of any teacher in the gym. If Ralph were to hit me, a teacher would be sure to see it. I had never fought back before from his taunting but picking on Chockie was too much.

Suddenly, Mrs. Richardson came between us, placing one hand out in front of each of us, like a police officer stopping traffic. "What's going on here?" she asked, turning her head to look at me and then Ralph.

I looked at Ralph and Ralph glared at me.

"Nothing," I said dejectedly. "Just a misunderstanding."

Mrs. Richardson took a moment to look at each of us. "Ralph, you go in the back of the other students to watch. Peter, you can resume your presentation." She nodded at me.

"His dumb fish wasn't doing anything. Dumb project. Dumb fish," Ralph said.

"Ralph, get back as I told you and keep your mouth closed," Mrs. Richardson ordered.

Ralph moved back behind the other students, which now numbered more than before. Some students came over when they heard and saw what was going on.

I was dumbfounded, not knowing how I could pull this off now. Chockie must be completely frightened. It was now even more embarrassing, seeing the bigger crowd, which now included Mrs. Richardson, who probably wanted to make certain there were no more disruptions.

I stood silently and swallowed hard, then looked back to Chockie, expecting to seal the fate of my project if he wouldn't move. To my surprise, Chockie was out of the corner, now hovering upright in the middle of the tank.

Rejuvenated, I pulled out the container of mealworms, and then I began again. I pushed one of the buttons and the middle ring lit. Chockie took notice and quickly swam through it.

Someone in the group said, "Did you see that?"

I dropped in a mealworm and Chockie snapped it up. When I pushed another button, a different ring lit, and Chockie swam through that one.

"Big deal," someone from the back said in a sarcastic voice.

I recognized the voice. I reached under the stand and took from one of the shelves a black box with numbers on it from 1 to 20. I showed the students the device, demonstrating how it lit up when I lightly pressed on one of the numbers. I placed it carefully inside the tank and hooked it on the back glass, so everyone could see each of the numbers.

I opened a door on the stand, took a deck of cards from a shelf, and then shuffled the cards. I fanned out the cards and offered them to a girl in the front row. "Take a card," I said. When she did, I asked a boy to take another card. "I want you to look at the cards, then hold them so that Chockie can see them."

They did so, showing a three of spades and a nine of diamonds.

"Chockie, I want you to add the two numbers of the two cards, then press the number that is the answer," I said.

Chockie came to the front glass, looking directly at the students and the cards. He swam stationary for a few moments, then quickly turned and pushed one of the numbers.

The number "12" lit up and the students offered many "wows" and spoke comments like, "That's a smart fish!"

Chockie and I repeated the demonstration, this time adding a 5 and a 10 for a total of 15, as Chockie indicated. Each time, I dropped in some mealworms as a reward. "This shows several things," I said in conclusion of my presentation. "For one, it shows that humans and animals can learn to communicate with one another. Secondly, it shows that animals can think in abstract terms and thirdly, they are more intelligent than what we give them credit for."

"That's crazy," came a voice from the back. It was from Ralph. "Fish can't do math. You must be cheating."

I wasn't expecting to be challenged. It was all so straight-forward for me, knowing all that Chockie could do. I took a moment before answering and cleared my throat, "No. I wasn't cheating. Chockie was doing all the math by himself," I said, then ended my demonstration so Ralph couldn't challenge him again by saying, "Thank you, everyone."

The students clapped and many of them were talking about Chockie as they walked away.

Jeannie lingered behind the rest of the crowd and approached me. "I like Chockie," she said. "He's really cute. How long have you had him?"

"Almost a year," I said, a little nervous but smiling.

Jeannie glanced at the group moving away. She gave a big smile to me. "Thanks for showing us. I have to go," she said, holding her clipboard tight to her chest. "Bye."

"Bye," I said, trying to think of something more I could say to keep her near me. I could think of nothing.

Mrs. Richardson approached me after Jeannie had left and told me how impressed she was with the project. I wondered if she said this to all the participants in the science fair or if she meant it.

Chockie and I repeated the same tasks two more times and always received a good response from the students. When the time was up, all the score sheets had been tallied and it was announced that Tiffany Smith got first place with her algae to fuel demonstration. Chockie and I got second place. I really thought Chockie was better than Tiffany's experiment, but at least the whole thing was over and I could take Chockie home.

Since it was near the end of the school day, the students could clear out their displays and then go home. Mitch and I placed Chockie back in a pail, siphoned the water back into pails, tore down the aquarium, filter, heater, and stand, then placed everything into Mitch's car.

His car was packed full and Mitch considered making two trips, but I said I wanted to get Chockie back home as soon as I could. I didn't want to go back to school for a second trip. Mitch agreed to my request, so we crammed everything around me, the fish tank in the back seat and the stand extruding from the open trunk. We were fully loaded.

Once we got back to my house, we unloaded Chockie, the pails of water, and my project lights. We dumped the water back into the Chockie's aquarium in my bedroom and then got Chockie back into his comfortable and familiar surroundings. Mitch congratulated me again for the second place and mostly, for Chockie's excellent performance, and then left for the pet shop to return everything.

I proudly draped a silver medal on a lanyard over Chockie's aquarium.

My mother came in and stood looking, with her hands on her hips, at the medal and Chockie, then at me. "Well done!" she said. "I'm so proud of you. Was it fun?"

"Yeah," I pondered whether I should say anything about the difficult start, but decided to forget about that part. "Yeah, it was fun. I was so proud of Chockie. He did so well – everything he had trained for."

"Chockie is quite special, isn't he?" she asked.

My pride and love for Chockie got the best of me. I tried to answer her, but I got choked up, a lump forming in my throat.

My mother smiled and hugged me until I recovered from my emotional moment. "Well, I'm so glad everything went so well. Dinner is in a half-hour," she said, walking through the doorway and pulling the door shut behind her.

After several minutes of resting on the bed while watching Chockie, I broke the silence., "You did great, Chockie. I know it wasn't easy for you. I know you were scared. How come you finally came out and performed?"

"I saw how you were being treated, and I wasn't doing what I needed to do. I realized I needed to help you," Chockie said.

"I appreciate that. Thank you," I said. "Did you get comfortable doing it after a while?"

"No. I didn't like it," Chockie said. "I felt like everyone was looking at me. I felt like a fish in a fishbowl."

At first, I was at a loss for words. Then the analogy struck me as funny.

"Um…" I laughed and said, "Yeah. I can see that."

CHAPTER 21

Talking is Easy for a Fish

⁓

"**H**OW DID YOU ever learn to talk like a human?" I asked Chockie. "You're a fish. Don't you have your own fish language?"

"Wait a minute. One question at a time," Chockie wiggled back and forth. "Fish are more intelligent than you people think. We have a way of learning languages quite fast. You just have to keep an open mind and be able to observe. As for your second question, yes, we do have our own way of talking. I don't know that you would call it a language, but it's more a way of communicating. You people rely so much on your ears, but we use a combination of sounds, body language, and vibrations. For instance, what do you think this means?"

He swam to the front glass flared his gills and pushed up against the glass with his lips, mouth wide, backed up and hit the glass again with his lips.

"I'd say that you're attacking the glass," I said.

"Right," Chockie answered, "but when I do that to another fish, it means 'back off – this is my territory.'"

"Yeah, I can see that."

"So, what does this mean?" Chockie assumed a vertical position, staring at the surface of the water and remaining motionless.

"Uh. I don't know."

"It means I'm hungry and I'm looking for food. Feed me."

"Oh, I see," I said.

"No, really. Feed me. I'm hungry," Chockie pleaded. "Please?"

"Oh, sure," I said with a laugh, then opened a container of food sticks and deposited a few sticks in the water.

Chockie snapped them up.

"Tell me more," I said. "How do you say, 'Help me with my homework'?"

"We don't know 'homework' because we don't have homework in our world. We swim around and eat each other, remember?"

"I suppose."

"But we do have a way of signaling for help. With all the danger out there, almost everything swimming around wants to eat us so occasionally we have to ask for help, especially when we're guarding the babies."

"So, how do you do it?"

"First you give a little, sharp, and forceful quake. Like this," Chockie said, then thrust his body like giving a sharp twitch. "That signals to the others that you mean business and there is danger nearby. Then you do this, "Rrrrr rrrrrr."

The sound was like a grinding noise.

"What was that?"

"It's back in my throat - like I'm chewing something. It's easy. You try it."

"Grrrr grrrr," I tried.

"No, deeper – in the throat. And you have to grind more. It's the vibrations in the water that other fish can hear."

"Grrgrrrgrgack!" I sounded.

"That's better. Now try doing it in the water. It sounds different in water than it does in the air."

"Nah. That's weird. I'm not sticking my head in the water. Yuk!"

"It's not so weird. Hey, this is my home you're degrading. All you have to do is put your lips in the water and make that sound. You want to learn fish talk, don't you? After all, I learned *your* language."

"Okay," I said reluctantly. I removed the aquarium top and set it vertical on the floor, resting against the wall. I bent my head over the aquarium, looking into the water. "You got to be kidding me."

"You'll be okay. Just don't inhale."

"Ha! You're funny." I placed my lips on the water and began making the sound. "Grrgrrrgrgack! Grrgrrrgrgack!" Air bubbled from my lips to the surface.

"Hey, that's pretty good. Try it once more, this time with a little more gusto."

"Grrgrrrgrgack! Grrgrrrgrgack!" I tried my best.

Without warning, the bedroom door swung open. "Oh my god, Peter! What are you doing?" my mother gasped. "Don't drink that water! Yuk! That will make you sick."

It took me a few seconds to think about what it looked like to her. "Oh. No, I wasn't drinking the water. I was talking to Chockie. In his language. I had to talk to him in water. It comes out differently."

"I see, "she said suspiciously. "What were you saying to him?"

"Help. That was the fish-way of saying help. He's going to teach me other words, too..." My voice trailed off, thinking how stupid it must have sounded.

"Uh-huh," my mother said. "I'm not sure what to think of that. Do you have your homework done?"

"Not quite."

"I thought so. Get it done. Then try cleaning up this pigsty. I can't even walk through this room. Pick up some of this stuff. Look at all those wrappers. You have a garbage can in here, you know."

"Yeah, I know. I'll get right to it."

My mother turned and shut the door behind her.

I listened and heard her footsteps trailing down the hallway. "You got me in trouble," I said.

"Nah, she's not upset about you talking to me. She just thinks you are crazy. She's more upset that you never clean your room and hardly ever get your homework done."

"Have you ever talked to her?"

"No. Why would I do that? That's why I have you," Chockie said.

"I see."

"Hey Peter, there's just one more thing," Chockie offered.

"Yeah, what is it?"

"You know how you sometimes get up in the middle of the night to go to the bathroom?"

"Yeah ..." I replied, not sure where he was going with this conversation.

"Could you not turn on the light? Fish don't have any eyelids like you people. When I am sleeping in the dark and suddenly, there is a bright light, it blinds me. It takes me quite a while to adjust to the light and, by that time, you're back and the light goes off. Then it takes me quite a while to get back to sleep."

"Oh, sorry. I didn't realize it bothered you."

"Maybe use a flashlight instead?" Chockie suggested.

"Deal." I nodded.

CHAPTER 22
Native American Storytelling

$\sim\!$

A S THE WINDS began to blow and the snow seemed to fall sideways more than down, cold weather set in. Winter in Wisconsin wasn't always kind or graceful and many people have surrendered to its cruelty. But for the most part, residents learned to live with the brutal aspects and make the best of whatever Mother Nature threw at them. Those who couldn't take the harshness moved to southern climates but, more often than not, they eventually returned. However, Wisconsin was in most residents' blood and the only way of life they knew, taking both the good and the bad.

This seemed to be one of the more mild winter days when Tommy invited me to spend an afternoon with him, as Tommy's family was planning to attend a winter culture camp that weekend. The camp was set up on Ho-Chunk grounds, providing an educational opportunity for everyone, especially the Ho-Chunk children who needed to learn more about their beliefs and customs.

I was especially interested in one part of the event. I wanted to listen to the ancient stories passed down from generation to generation. I'd heard bits and pieces of stories, mostly from Tommy, but no one was allowed to repeat the stories unless that person had the stories memorized in the exact words. This requirement ensured the stories wouldn't be changed through time. Also, it was mostly elders who told the stories.

By the cultural rules, storytelling could only take place in winter when there was snow on the ground so this severely limited me the opportunity to hear them.

Tommy, his father, mother, brother, sister, and I all rode in the family's minivan. As we drew near to the grounds, I could see the smoke rising into the air from the wood fire and the numerous tents set up with many people scattered about the grounds. One of the structures was called a ciiporike, pronounced "chip-po-tik-kay," also known as a wigwam, a long building with an arched roof and flat ends. The arched roof was made from saplings stuck into the ground on one side, then bent in an arch and the other end stuck into the ground on the other side. This method continued for the entire length of the building and then they covered it with whatever natural material found, which could be animal hides, pine boughs, or whatever covering could be found. This was built in the traditional materials and methods from ancient days, Tommy told me.

Tommy's family and I piled out of the vehicle after we pulled into a parking spot. I didn't know anyone else there, but Tommy's father and mother were halted frequently on their walk to the camp by people they knew and wanted to exchange greetings.

One person was Tommy's uncle Ben, whom Tommy called Tega, which sounded more like "Degga." It was a Ho-Chunk term for an uncle who makes sure the nephew grew up with the correct cultural teachings and administered discipline when necessary. However, in Ho-Chunk culture, a child had no uncles or aunts. They are considered their fathers and mothers, I learned.

Ben joined us as we walked into the grounds.

"Tega, this is my friend, Peter," Tommy said to Ben.

Ben held out his hand to me. "It's nice to meet you."

"Nice to meet you," I replied as I shook his hand.

We visited a station where a man demonstrated how to flesh a deer hide, removing the fat with a knife from the underside of the skin. Behind him was a stretched hide on a rack made of poplar poles. Leather straps were pulled tightly around the frame and through holes placed along the edges of the pelt.

Inside one of the tents, an elderly woman demonstrated how to make moccasins from tanned deer hides. She explained the tanning process, which involved soaking the hide in deer brains, which made the skin into soft and pliable leather. Once the pieces were cut and assembled into moccasins, they were adorned with intricate beadwork, which made them into beautiful works of art.

We went on to another tent, where a wood-carving demonstration was taking place. Some male elders had taken sections of trees, cut them down into more manageable blocks of wood, and then carved them with hand tools. The result was wooden bowls and spoons with the very fine and intricate grain.

Many young boys were lined up to play 'Snow Snake,' a game where the children would throw a carved straight stick down a 300-foot channel of snow. The child who could slide it down the channel the furthest was declared the winner.

I'd gotten anxious to head into the ciiporike where the stories were being told. When we entered through an end door, we noticed it was much darker inside and it took a couple of minutes for our eyes to adjust to the dim light. We found spots to sit on the ground along the outer edges of the structure and listened to the elder sitting in the middle at the end of the building. He spoke with a deep, serious voice and I wondered if it would hypnotize me.

Several stories were told, many of them considered "creation stories," about how the Creator made them and how the Ho-Chunk people were on Earth when dinosaurs were in existence and during the Ice Age.

When the storytelling was over, I felt frustrated that I'd heard nothing about the animals talking many years ago, so when I was walking with Ben, I asked him if animals could talk at one time and if it could happen again.

Ben stood and thought deeply before answering, "Yes, there are stories of animals talking, but not in the verbal sense. Animals don't have the vocal cords to be able to speak like humans. Rather, it has been said that animals can read our thoughts. If you look at civilizations throughout history, all have common rituals of people humbling themselves to be able to connect with the Creator, whether it's starving, or inflicting pain such as piercing, or hangings from the skin or whatever means. It's when people have been humbled and lower themselves to be able to see or hear or otherwise communicate with spirits of the Creator. In that manner, they have to have everything removed from their minds and be able to see things on a very basic and primitive level. Babies have that innocence because they have not yet acquired other thoughts other than pure innocence and are accepting of everything given to them. They take everything for what it is on a most basic level. That's why it is often said they can see things, such as spirits, that adults can't. That's why babies aren't allowed to attend funerals and other similar ceremonies."

I listened and understood most of what he was saying.

"So, back to your original question," Ben went on. "It has been told that animals could communicate with people at one time. People had respect for animals, as the Creator had intended. It used to be that when we hunted, we only did so to feed our families and the animals understood that. When a kill was made, we prayed and thanked the animal for giving its life for us. When the white man showed up, many times animals were killed for the sake of sport, and people had no respect or reverence for the animal. It's then when the animal came to fear man and then the line of communication was broken. So in theory, yes, animals could communicate with us again, but only when we humble ourselves and we have no preconceived notions or plan."

I looked at Ben's eyes with undying gratitude. He had just explained something I had wondered about in earnest ever since Chockie started talking to me. I respected his words of wisdom. "Oh," I said, thoughts turning over in my head. "Thank you. Thank you so much. You have given me a lot to think about."

CHAPTER 23

Thoughts About Jeannie

~⁀

HOMEWORK WAS NEVER a priority for me. It felt like more of a chore than anything and I procrastinated doing it as long as I could. I could play on my Xbox, text my friends, and find a million other things to do other than my school assignments. Finally, around 9 o'clock, I gathered my materials and sat at a little table in my room to start completing the arduous tasks.

Algebra took a lot of concentration, something in short supply tonight. My mind kept wandering and I often resorted to sketching characters on scratch paper. I liked to draw fish, in particular Chockie, but sometimes I drew people, too. I was drawing the face of a young girl, one with long hair and almond-shaped eyes when I began to talk to myself without realizing it, "Oh Jeannie, you are so beautiful," I said softly.

"Jeannie?" Chockie said loudly. "Who is Jeannie? I've heard you mention that name before."

I tapped the eraser end of my pencil firmly on my paper, irritated at the question. "Shut up, Chockie," I fired back.

"It's none of your business." I surprised myself by talking aloud and embarrassed that Chockie had heard it. I started to wonder just how much I actually said.

"Sorry," Chockie said in concession. "I didn't know you were so sensitive about it. I must have hit a nerve."

I realized I'd overreacted, letting out a huge sigh. "I'm sorry, Chockie. I didn't mean to yell at you. She's just a girl in my grade," I said.

"You said she is beautiful. You like her, don't you?"

"Sort of," I muttered with my head down, scratching at the paper with my pencil.

"Yeah, I can tell. What is she like?"

"I'd rather not talk about her right now. I have homework to do, you know."

"Yes. I see that."

I pretended to work at my homework for a little while before my defenses came down. "She has long blond hair and the most incredible eyes I've ever seen. Her voice is so soft and wonderful." I stared blankly up at the ceiling and smiled, lost somewhere between the moon and the stars.

"Sounds nice. Does she like you, too?"

"I think so. She does talk to me once in a while. But I really don't know for certain," I said, returning to the present and looking down at my paper.

"Don't be shy, Peter. You need to let her know how you feel. We have a saying with the guys in the fish world that if you don't do the side slap, she'll never know that you like her. But before you do that, you need to send her little signals so she has clues that you like her."

"Clues? Like what? What kind of clues?"

"You know, like to swim beside her and do a little twitch."

Chockie gave a demonstration by staying in one spot in the water while wiggling his body.

"Now how do you suppose I'm going to do that? I'm not a fish and we don't live in the water. I'd look pretty foolish trying that. I'd only get laughed at." I shook my head.

"Well, there are things we say, too. It's what you people call flirting. You say something and then see what kind of reaction you get. If she looks happy, then you know you're on the right track."

"Like what?"

"Oh, we say stuff like, 'Hey girl, you sure do have beautiful fins,' or 'I sure like your wake because I'd follow you anywhere,' or make small talk like, 'Did you see those new shrimp in the pond?'"

I thought about what Chockie said and soon dismissed them. "Nah, I don't think any of them would work with a human girl. Got anything else?"

Chockie was silent for a few moments. "Well, when I want to see a girl fish again, when I am leaving her I'll say, 'Don't hide in the weeds,' so she knows I want to see her again. That always works."

"Ah, I don't think any of that would work on Jeannie."

"Try it. Works every time for fish. You never know unless you try something. Be bold."

"Yeah, maybe I'll think up something on my own. I don't think your fish words translate to human language too well."

"Suit yourself. Just let her know how you feel. You can never go wrong with that."

"I suppose." I thought for a moment, then glanced at the clock. "Now let me get my homework done. It's almost bedtime."

"Should have let me do it. I would have had it done hours ago," Chockie said.

I smiled at the thought, knowing he couldn't really do it. "Yeah, but my teachers won't take waterlogged paper homework written by a fish." I laughed. "Besides, your penmanship is terrible."

CHAPTER 24
Hidden Pain

I SAW HIM BEFORE my dad did. It immediately caused my chest to tighten up. "Dad, let's go this way," I said.

"Why?" my father asked as he continued on his path down the aisle at the local grocery store.

I desperately pulled on my father's arm while keeping my eyes on the man further down the row who was picking up a jar of peanut butter or something. I noticed him right away, but obviously, my dad had not.

"Just a minute. We need something down here," my father said, never breaking stride.

Maybe our conversation alerted the man, but it didn't matter. He would have seen us eventually anyway as long as we continued down the aisle. The man lowered his hand, letting the jar of peanut butter hang at his side. I could see his body straightened up.

My dad stopped suddenly with his eyes locked on the man down the aisle.

At that moment, time stopped. My dad and the man stared at each other.

I was afraid of what might happen next. To me, the man dressed in a faded and well-worn brown jacket looked like a bear. His crew-cut hair and neck the same width of his head made him look like a football player. He looked twice the size of my father and twice as mean.

I had seen him before. I knew him as Ralph's father.

"Brighton," Ralph's dad said, finally breaking the silence.

"Greg," my dad said in return, his eyes diverting from the big man, turning his head and looking down at me. He looked back at the man, nodded his head sharply, and then turned around. "Let's go," he said to me.

"Just a minute, Brighton," the booming voice said.

My dad stopped in his tracks and paused for a second before turning around. He didn't say a word.

Ralph's father looked like he began to say something, but paused and then looked briefly at me. "Have a good day."

It sounded more sarcastic to me. I don't think he meant it. I looked at the man's huge hand, holding that jar of peanut butter, and saw that it was chapped and rugged, big enough to grasp a basketball with just that one hand.

It looked like he was about to squeeze the jar until it popped. The man's eyes darted to my father and then back to me. His face and body relaxed. He paused for another second and then placed the peanut butter in his cart.

My dad turned around. "Come on. Let's go," my dad said.

I noticed my father's gait was a little faster and I had to walk quickly to keep up with him.

Zipping into an open self-checkout counter, he scanned the items and threw them into paper bags in random order. I was almost certain we would arrive home with some broken eggs.

I felt safer outside the store, not that anything would happen inside the store, but at least the tension was less. The groceries were loaded into the trunk of my dad's spotless red '68 Mustang convertible and I climbed inside. When my father grabbed the driver's side door handle, he paused for a moment, staring at the top of the left fender. He went to the spot where he was looking and rubbed lightly with his forefinger. While he was rubbing the spot, I noticed the many scars crisscrossing on both his arms. I had seen them before and always wondered how he got them. For some reason, they stood out now. He had another on his neck and I sort-of forgot about that one too, but now it was brought back to my attention.

Satisfied the peculiar spot was rubbed off and wasn't anything permanent, he returned to the door and climbed in.

I often wondered why he paid so much attention to his car while other things went unattended around the house. It was as if he loved the car more than anything else. I didn't feel comfortable asking my father about what just happened, so I sat quietly and intended to remain quiet for the rest of the ride.

He drove with his right hand on the steering wheel, his left arm resting on the window ledge.

Riding in his convertible with the top down was usually fun, the wind tossing my hair in every direction and the warm sun shining down on me. But this time, I was distracted. I was thinking about my father and what conflict might be going on in his mind.

Instead of heading straight home, my father took a right

turn onto a rural blacktop road that went past many family dairy farms.

When the road was flat and void of any cars, my dad stepped down on the accelerator pedal. The car hesitated for a moment before taking off like a bullet, forcing me against the back of my seat.

"Darn timing must be off," my father muttered to himself. "I've been through the carburetor a hundred times. It can't be that."

I didn't say anything.

We took a longer route home, with my father testing the car several times more until we reached our driveway. The garage door opened and we rolled in. As soon as the car stopped in the garage, my father was out and opened the hood.

I decided to leave him alone. "I'll take the groceries in," I said, but got no reply. I wasn't sure if he heard me or not, but I opened the trunk, grabbed the grocery bag, and entered the house.

"Hi Honey," my mom said to me as I set the bag on the kitchen counter. "How was your trip?"

"Interesting."

"Why is that, if I may ask?" She was folding clothes from the dryer on the kitchen table.

"Mr. Higgins was there," I said.

Immediately my mother's expression went from a smile to a more serious look. "Oh, no. What—what happened? Did they talk to each other?"

"Oh yeah, they talked to each other," I said. "Well, I'm not sure you could call that talk."

My mother put her open hand to her mouth.

"Aw, it was nothing, really," I said. "They just looked at

each other but nothing happened. It's kind of scary, though. I didn't know what was going to happen."

"I'm sure nothing serious will ever happen," my mother assured me. "It never does."

I wondered what she meant because it sounded like this type of thing happened before.

"Did you get everything on the list?" she asked.

"Yeah, we did. But I was kind of hoping to get some Crater Puffs, but we had to make an early exit. Besides, Dad seemed to be in a hurry to work on his car. I don't know what is so important about that thing."

"He loves that car, that's for sure," my mother said while putting the eggs into the refrigerator. "I have a feeling it's his way of escaping from the rest of the world."

I thought about that for a minute, wondering if I wasn't so different from my father. Often I, too, have tried to escape from reality. It was always safer there.

CHAPTER 25

Hockey Danger

~~~∂

T HE WINDS OF change brought in cold, blustery days, and especially harsh nights. The wind could be heard howling and I tried to drown out the outside noise with gunfire from an Xbox game.

Snow came down in heavy sheets, piling up wherever it could, and then being tossed from place to place like some unwanted child of the clouds. Drifts piled up high behind the house and garage then even out into the roadways, causing major headaches for roadway clearing crews. Snowplows with flashing lights often drove by our house, trying to keep up with winter's fury.

School had to be canceled for two days in a row because of the blizzard, much to the liking of most, if not all, students. I know I certainly enjoyed the days away from school.

With a break in the many days of bad weather, the sun finally peaked out and mirrored its bright light off the reflective white snow that covered everything.

Tommy called me Sunday morning to see if I was doing anything.

"Not really," I said. "Why?"

"Well, there's a bunch of us planning to go to the Mill Pond and play some hockey. The city cleared off a spot for ice skating, so Jim and Sean and Henry and I wanted to try out our new hockey stuff. They have nets set up and everything. Want to come along?"

"Nah. I got things to do here. I got to change Chockie's water and some other stuff."

"That can wait until you get home. We're only going to be out there for a couple of hours. Besides, I think Zeke plans to be there and his sister Jeannie might come along."

He knew of my attraction to Jeannie and I don't know if he was teasing me or using her name to get me to come along.

"Well, can you come?" Tommy asked.

"I don't have any equipment. All I have are ice skates," I said.

"That's okay. We have a ton of hockey sticks in the garage. My brothers always played hockey when they were around," Tommy said, then listened to a long pause of the line, waiting for me to say something. "Come on. It'll be fun."

"Oh, alright."

"Good. My mom is driving, so we'll pick you up in about a half-hour. Ok?

"Yeah. Ok."

I told my mother that I was going, found my ice skates in the basement, got bundled up, and went outside to wait for Tommy and his mother to pick me up.

"Where are you going?" my father asked while shoveling

snow near the front door. He had cleared the driveway with his garden tractor and blade, but now was clearing the walkways from the house by hand.

"Tommy invited me to play some hockey down on the Mill Pond," I replied while twirling the skates suspended by the shoestrings.

"Ok, but be careful," my father said. "I used to skate on that pond, too, when I was young. The ice can be thin in some spots because of the current underneath. Some of us learned the hard way."

"You used to play hockey on that pond?"

"Yeah. Sometimes it got kind of rough," he said, leaning on his shovel and staring across the road while in thought. "But it was fun – some of the best times of my life. I remember when I shot the puck from the back goal and it skipped across the top of Timmy Krause's head and went into the goal at the other end. Everyone died laughing. It was the craziest thing anyone had ever seen."

A car came roaring down the road and came to a stop at the end of the driveway. It was Tommy and his mother.

I looked at my dad and smiled. "Well, see you later," I said, and then turned and trotted to the waiting car.

"Have fun," my father shouted.

Many of the roads held a compacted layer of snow, a layer that wouldn't go away until the next thaw, which would be a few months. Meanwhile, everyone adjusted to winter driving, knowing a slide was possible at any moment and controlling it became second nature, my dad always said... just part of life in Wisconsin.

Margret pulled to the side of the road near the edge of Mill Pond, aptly named for a gristmill that used to operate a few feet downside of the spillway. The spillway blocked the water flowing down Douglas Creek, forming Mill Pond.

Remnants of the mill still stood but deteriorated badly with the wheel rotted, removed, and placed inside. I had heard many discussions about restoring the historic structure, but talk is all that ever happened. The local newspaper reported that money was needed and the estimates always were more than what residents were able to collect from donations.

When we pulled to a stop beside Mill Pond, I could see there were about seven kids out on the ice, scrambling around on their skates. On occasion, I saw some of them go down on the ice, feet flying out from under them and landing on their posteriors. Another car pulled up behind us when Tommy and I were climbing out of the car. Tommy handed me one of the hockey sticks and then he said goodbye to his mother. In the car behind us, three kids climbed out of the vehicle and they walked down a short path of packed snow before stepping onto the ice.

"Hey, Peter," one of them called out.

I looked to see Zeke raising his hockey stick in the air to me. A quick look behind him and I saw Jeannie stood there, too. I suddenly became a little nervous. "Hi Zeke," I yelled back, but my eyes immediately went to Jeannie. She smiled at me and I melted. I couldn't say anything no matter how much I wanted to.

"Hi Peter," she called out to me.

I was awe-stricken. I thought maybe I might pass out. "Hi," is all I could say. I immediately felt dumb for getting caught staring at her, blushed, and looked down at the snow in the path ahead of me.

As we got closer to the kids already playing on the ice, we could see a large oval had been cleared to make the perfect rink for skating. Snowbanks rimmed the edges of the rink, providing the boundaries for a hockey game, which helped to keep the puck from going astray. Two homemade PVC pipe goals had been made and were in place, sitting on each end of the oval.

We saw nowhere to sit, so just like the rest of the kids now arriving, Tommy and I sat on a hard-packed area of the snowbank where it looked like other kids had done the same thing. We took off our boots and pulled on our skates. Tying the skates was the hardest part and the most important. I knew from the other times I skated that the laces had to be extra tight so there wasn't any slop. If it was tight, my ankle wouldn't turn over, which is always a problem when trying to balance on those thin metal blades.

Testing out the fit and my abilities, I stood up on my skates to wiggle and wobble onto the ice.

Tommy soon did the same.

My legs were a little wobbly as I tested the skates, making a few jaunts out onto the ice and then back.

Tommy and a few other boys soon joined me as we did some fancy slides near the end of the rink. As we grew accustomed to the skates, ice, and our abilities, our speed picked up and our moves became more confident.

"Come on Peter! Let's get in the game," Tommy shouted, heading to the other end of the ice skating area. Other kids were slapping their hockey sticks on the ice in an attempt to emulate Wayne Gretzky, sending the puck flying a foot off the ice surface and into the net.

When several more boys arrived, we split up into teams, with each team separating and moving to opposite ends of the ice rink. While skating around, getting ready to start the game, my ears picked up a familiar voice. At the other end of the ice rink was a bigger kid, guarding the goal with full pads and a face mask, although it looked more like a baseball catcher's facemask than a hockey one. More barking orders confirmed my suspicions.

Ralph.

I set it in my mind that he would stay in the goal and not come over to the open area of the ice rink. Since Ralph was on the other team, the main objective would be to put the puck in the goal Ralph was defending. I'd rather just skate on the other end of the ice and stay away from him. I'd help defend our own goal.

I wasn't sure if Ralph saw me or not. It shouldn't matter since he'd be busy with his job as a goaltender and he might leave me alone. He should be preoccupied with playing the game, anyway. *Hopefully.*

One of the guys agreed to drop the puck in the middle of the ice and it resulted in the mad slashing of sticks with the puck flying in all directions like a steel ball in a pinball machine.

Skates slashed into the ice, spraying tiny ice chips away from the blades and producing a slicing sound. Kids dashed around the rink, some following the puck while others hung back, waiting for a pass or to defend their goal.

I stayed back, trying to avoid crossing over to the other end and not going anywhere near Ralph.

A shot sent the puck down toward me, heading for the goal guarded by Jake Spiegel. I skated towards it, but I saw that Jake had it well in hand so I circled behind the net. I was a little surprised when Jake dished the puck off to me as I came around the other side. I took the puck and dribbled it forward, skating up the right side of the rink.

A group of three or four defenders came skating toward me from the other side in a curtain wall of death. My eyes quickly shifted from side to side, looking for someone to pass the puck to.

Zeke was shouting to me at the left side of the rink as I

skated parallel to him. He was alone, while members of the other team were rushing toward me.

I pulled back my stick and made a slap shot that would have made any NHL coach proud. However, the puck never reached its intended target, bouncing off a player's skate or two and making a sharp right. The puck flew toward Ralph and before he had time to react, slid by him and into the back of the net.

"Wooo hooo!" members of my team yelled out and came over to slap me on the back and congratulate me.

I was mobbed for a minute or so, and then they all dispensed to get ready for the next puck drop. My eyes went to the goal, amazed that my pass turned into a goal. Standing there in front of the goal was Ralph, his eyes piercing into me. I did not doubt it now. Ralph knew I was there.

I retreated to my left side again, preparing in case another puck was sent my way. The puck was dropped at center ice and the sticks again began the rhythm of clicking on the ice surface. The puck flew back to the right side where Killian was waiting, but the onslaught of aggressive skaters was upon him before he knew it. Several players slapped the puck around furiously until it was in front of our goal, with Jake madly trying to grab or sit on the thing. He did eventually trap the puck under his leg, although it took a few moments before the other team stopped pounding on it, trying to break the puck free.

Jake waited for the area to clear and then dished the puck off to Johnny, on our team, who sped down the ice with the puck sliding ahead of his stick. Johnny skated down the side and crossed over to the middle to make a shot on the goal, but before he could, several sticks slammed at the puck and into his legs, causing him to go down and hit the ice hard.

None of us were wearing helmets since none of us were

serious hockey players. I think he may have hit his head. Johnny laid on the ice, moaning in pain and all the action stopped. A couple of the boys went over, picked him up under his arms, and carried him to the side. He sat on the snowbank where a couple of the moms looked after him.

"Peter," Killian said, who was our leader on the team, "can you take Johnny's place? We need someone to play forward. You can do it."

"Well …" I stared at Ralph standing at the goal. I didn't want to get that close to him, but at the same time, I didn't want to say no to Killian. "I guess so …"

"Good. You can take up his position on the right side."

I just made it to the right side, just in the back of the centerline, as the puck was dropped. The puck flew to the opposite side of the rink, then shuffled down toward my team's goal. It was met with a flurry of the clacking of sticks, often with wood striking flesh and bone and the cries of sudden angry pain.

Suddenly, a combination of hard slams caused the puck to fly high through the air right at me. Moving aside, I watched the track of the puck and backed up slightly as the puck landed near my skates. I was standing alone, several yards from the nearest player, but I knew they would be coming at me in a few seconds.

My stick cupped the puck and I slid it forward as I skated toward the goal with only the goalie, Ralph, between me and the net.

When I got within five feet of Ralph, I skated past Ralph, then slapped the puck backward with the backside of my stick. Ralph wasn't expecting the shot and suddenly flailed his arms and legs when he saw the puck coming, but the puck sailed past his right side and into the goal.

A loud cheer from my teammates erupted, yelling, "Peter! Peter! Peter!"

Ralph's face turned into an angry frown and he slammed his hockey stick down flat on the ice. "That's the last time you're going to do that, Peter!" Ralph shouted.

I wasn't sure what he intended to do, but I didn't want to wait around to find out. I quickly skated toward the opposite side of the ice as fast as I could. I didn't see what was going on because my back was turned, but I rotated around just in time to see Ralph pick up his hockey stick off the ice and fling it at me. The other players yelled and I avoided getting hit, but his hockey stick flew out onto the snow well beyond the ice.

"Okay, let's take a break, guys," Killian shouted across the ice. "End of the period. Everyone take 10 minutes."

I was congratulated as my team and I met up on the right side of the rink. Then many players sat down for a few minutes on the snowbank to rest while the other team took to the left side of the rink.

That is, everyone except Ralph, who was still fuming as he trudged through the snow to retrieve his hockey stick which traveled about 30 feet from the rink. We all watched as he made the trek.

Many of the players were drinking water, removing their skates to rest their ankles and feet, talking to each other when a loud crack sounded throughout the cold air. Everyone's head turned, looking for the source of the noise.

Some of the players saw what happened next while others missed it completely. Ralph suddenly disappeared from view. Several gasps erupted from those who saw it. Trying to comprehend what they just saw, most everyone stood and stared in the direction of Ralph's last sighting.

When people realized what happened, a mad flurry of

talk emanated from the players, with finally some players running as fast as they could toward where Ralph was last seen. A group of three players stopped short, looking at the broken pieces of ice a few feet ahead.

I caught up with the three boys and stood as close as we could safely, wondering what to do. We stared at the open water in the middle, expecting Ralph to appear. Broken ice slabs bobbed in the hole and water had been splashed upon the surrounding snow.

Eventually, Ralph's head and arms emerged from the hole, a gasp for air breaking the silence and his hands flailing, trying to clutch anything on the sides. The effort was futile, as Ralph could not grasp anything substantial, or even maintain his head above water for very long. He slipped back under the surface.

"Somebody do something!" a voice called out.

"Call 9-1-1!" one of the boys yelled back to the rink, hoping one of the parents had a cell phone available.

My eyes were glued to the open water, wondering if Ralph would come back up, or if he was gone forever. I knew that if he came up, it wouldn't be for very long. No doubt, he couldn't stay in that cold water for very long. There was no time to waste. My heart was pounding loudly and fast with my mind racing on what to do next. I laid down on the snow and inched myself closer to the open water.

"No, Peter! Don't get too close! The ice is thin and you'll fall in, too!" one of the boys yelled. I think it was Johnny's voice.

I slipped myself closer, hoping the ice would not give out beneath me. I slid forward until I got to the edge of the water. I figured he might have one last chance to come up to the top.

I was right.

Ralph's head and arms came exploding through the water, hands flailing in panic, reaching for anything he could grab, but facing the opposite way. Loud gasps emanated from his mouth while he tried to get air back into his lungs. I reached as far as I could, grasping his jacket on the shoulder and pulling him closer.

By this time, two of the boys had come up behind me, also lying prone next to the broken ice, holding onto my legs, so I wouldn't fall into the water, too.

Ralph must have felt my tug on his jacket and he whirled around in the water, his hands closing on my outstretched arms. I pulled him closer and Ralph held tight on the sleeves of my jacket. The two boys who were holding on my legs began to pull me away from the open hole and along with Ralph, who came out of the water up to his waist. Then the boys gave an extra effort, fully pulling me with Ralph coming completely out the water. We were lying there, both exhausted until some of the kids grasped Ralph and got him far enough away from the hole.

I continued to recover, breathing heavily. I was about to crawl backward when I felt something under me move.

Ralph had been pulled far enough inward so he was safe, but there wasn't enough time for me to get out of there.

I had no time to react. It happened so suddenly, I didn't realize what happened until I felt myself falling through the ice and into the frigid water.

I shut my eyes as I felt the water crash all around me and envelop my body. I opened my eyes and I could see the bright surface above me moving away as I plunged deeper into the depths of the dark water below.

My body felt heavy. My skates, water-soaked jacket, and clothes instantly became added weight, pulling me downward as I struggled to rise back to the surface.

I kicked with my feet and used my arms and hands to move me upward, all the while holding my breath. When I finally reached the top, I felt like my lungs were going to explode. I was hoping to find my way to the top, maybe to grasp something – maybe a hand from someone at the top – to get out of the water. My lungs were burning and I didn't know how to get air. I was beginning to panic.

I made a final effort, propelling myself upward, but my head struck something hard. It took me a few seconds to understand that I had not come straight up and I missed the hole as I swam up. My head hit the bottom of the ice. I immediately began to thrash about, looking for open water. I tried to move sideways, searching for the brighter light from the surface that would indicate an opening in the ice.

My body was weakening and I began to sink lower in the water, even though I was giving it all the effort I had left. As I was sinking, I saw a fish swim by me and fade into the distance. A walleye, or something like that, I figured. Then another fish came swimming up to me. And then another. Soon there was a school of fish, about 50 of them, all gathered around me.

I figured I must be hallucinating. My energy was gone. I felt exhausted. I couldn't hold my breath any longer and I released what air I had. Bubbles came from my mouth and rose toward the surface.

Suddenly, Chockie swam up to my face, about two feet away.

"Peter," Chockie said. "You can't give up. So many people love you. You need to try again."

"I can't, Chockie," I said, my vision blurring. I knew I was close to passing out. "I don't have the energy to go on."

"You do, Peter. There are no obstacles that you can't

overcome. You are my friend and I know you are capable of much more."

"But … how? What do I do?"

"What did I teach you?"

I thought for a moment. Then I let out a "Grrgrrrgrgack! Grrgrrrgrgack!"

The fish around me gathered closer. They pushed their mouths against me and began pushing me upward in the water. There seemed to be a hundred or more fish all around me, pushing on me all over my body. I saw the light above growing closer, first slowly, and then it seemed like I was gaining speed. The light above was coming at me at a furious pace.

I could hardly believe it. The fish were helping me. Somehow, all the pain had gone away. My lungs were no longer burning and I felt relaxed like a huge burden had lifted from me.

I entered into a bright white light and I was fine. I was at peace. Then, my vision went black—I lost consciousness.

CHAPTER 26
A Place for Healing

~

THAT CONSTANT BEEPING was annoying. I wished someone would shut it off. Also, there was a hissing sound, but I couldn't quite figure out what that was about, either.

I tried opening my eyes, but my eyelids were very heavy.

"I think he's coming out of it," a woman's voice said.

I fought to open my eyes. As I struggled to keep them open, I saw a woman I never saw before standing beside my bed. Next, I realized it wasn't my bed. I was somewhere else and it all seemed strange to me. I thought I was waking up in the morning at home, but nothing looked familiar.

I fought my groggy feeling and opened my eyes as best I could.

My mother quickly came into view, taking the place of the other woman.

Behind my mom, I could see Dad. "Where am I?" I asked, with my voice sounding muffled. I realized I was wearing something over my nose and mouth. I pulled the thing from my face and let it fall to the side. I took a quick look around the room and then I was able to understand where I was.

"You're in the hospital, Honey," my mother said tearfully. She clutched a handkerchief in one hand and placed her other hand against my cheek. "Oh god, I'm so happy you're awake. You had me so worried." Her tears were running down her cheeks.

"I'm okay, Mom," I said, looking at the crook of my arm with a wrapping of bandages and a line coming out of it. The line ran to a machine on a stand beside the bed. I started to remember what happened. "Ralph?" I asked. "Is he all right?"

"Yes, he is," my mom said. "Honey, thanks to you. You are a hero. You saved his life."

I turned my head away, looking down at my hand. "I'm not a hero."

"Everyone believes that you are, Peter. Never mind that right now. How are you feeling?"

At that moment, a doctor came through the door followed by the same nurse as before. "Ah, good," the doctor said, now standing at my left side with his hands on his hips. "You decided that you had enough sleep?" he asked with a big smile.

I didn't answer. I didn't know what to say.

The nurse turned off the oxygen by hitting a valve on the wall with her palm and removed the mask from around my neck.

The doctor took out a small light from his pocket and began to look into my eyes, then quickly placed the light back in his breast pocket. "You had quite a close call. We're all glad you made it through it. Now, let's concentrate on making you better." The doctor looked in my mouth and performed a few other tests. "We're going to keep you here tonight so we can keep an eye on you. It all looks pretty good, but we just have to make sure. I just want to make sure you don't develop pneumonia. You had quite a lot of water in your lungs when you first came in. If there are no problems, I'm fairly sure you will be able to go home tomorrow."

The doctor stood for a moment in silence, staring at me.

I felt strange to be stared at so closely.

He finally placed his hand on my arm. "You're a lucky boy. It's a miracle," he said. "Someone must be watching over you." He backed away from my bed. "I'll be back to check on you later." He nodded toward my parents, then turned and left the room.

The nurse stayed for a few moments to check that my IV solution was flowing at the correct rate and straightened the lines so they weren't twisted. Connecting another plastic tubing to the oxygen outlet on the wall, she placed the tubing just beneath my nose so that oxygen was flowing up into my nostrils. She handed me the remote and told me how to use the nurse-call button and the television, then left the room.

My mother slid her chair up close beside me and held my hand as her eyes glistened.

I could see the love and concern in her weary eyes. She looked as if she was stressed.

"I don't even know what to say, Peter. I have been praying to God for you to be okay and He came through for you. I-I was so scared…" Her voice trembled.

I looked off into the distance, blinking back the tears. I always got choked up when I saw my mother crying. Instead, I tried to concentrate on recalling what happened before I ended up in the hospital. I remembered up to the point I helped pull Ralph out of the water and I fell through the ice. But the other parts were coming back to me in bits and pieces. "Chockie!" I said suddenly, remembering that Chockie had appeared to me while I was underwater.

"Chockie is fine, dear. He's at home in your bedroom, anxious for you to return home."

"No, I mean, I saw Chockie in the pond. He helped me get out."

A puzzled look appeared on my mother's face and she turned to look at my father. My dad gave her a look of uncertainty and shrugged his shoulders, so my mom turned back to look at me.

"Just relax, Peter," my dad said. "You've been through a lot and you need to get some rest. Don't worry about Chockie. He's fine."

"No, I'm telling you, he was there with me. He helped me out of the water." I was growing agitated because I saw that they didn't believe me. "He reminded me that I could call for help and I did. Then all the fish in the pond pushed me up to the surface. I don't remember anything after that. But I'm telling you, it was Chockie and the other fish who saved my life!"

"Okay, okay, calm down Peter. I believe you. We'll talk about this later. The important thing is that you're alright," my mother said, then glancing again to look again at Dad. "I'm glad that Chockie could help you."

A nurse came into the room to check my vitals and talk to my parents. The nurse told them that I was still weak and perhaps they could come back later after I had more sleep.

"We're going to leave now, so you can get some rest. You've been through a terrible ordeal and we have to follow the doctor's orders. We'll be back in a couple of hours or so to check on you, okay?"

I let out a big sigh.

My mother told me that Tommy called and he was very worried about me. The first chance he got, he was going to come to visit me.

She helped me turn on the television and find the Animal Planet channel, which was my favorite. One of the staff came in and asked me what I wanted for dinner, so my mother and father must have thought it was good timing for them to slip out the door.

"We'll be back in a little while, okay? We're going to get something to eat and then we'll be right back. The important thing is that you relax."

"Okay," I said, pulling the sheet up to my neck and slumping down in the bed. "See you later."

My mother's eyes began to get teary again as she gripped my hand.

My father saw she was having an emotional moment so he put his arm around her shoulder. She turned to him and they embraced. My father's eyes squeezed tightly. They briefly kissed and turned their attention back to me.

"Honey, we are so glad you are okay. We love you so much," my mother said.

I saw that they were holding hands as they left the room. I'd never seen that before.

I knew my story about Chockie saving me sounded outlandish and perhaps I would never convince them of what really happened. I couldn't explain it either, but I knew what I experienced and I firmly believed Chockie had been there to help me.

After my parents left, I drifted off to sleep for a little while until a man showed up with a tray of food. I didn't eat much and then fell back asleep.

When my parents came back a little while later, I woke

up but I was groggy, so they decided to leave and come back in the morning.

I must have slept for several hours when I was awakened by a nurse. She wanted me to blow in a plastic device to raise a little blue ball inside. She explained it was to exercise my lungs so I wouldn't get pneumonia.

I understood and did it, even though I didn't feel like doing it.

Because of this, I was fully awake and I wanted to get out of bed for a while. I was restless and I felt like looking around. I swung my legs to the side of the bed and sat up, unhooked the sensor from my finger, took off the oxygen tubing, gathered the IV line, and stood up. Taking the portable IV tree with me in one hand, I wheeled it about the room, checking out all the drawers and cabinets. The opening in the back of the hospital gown was really bothering me.

I found nothing particularly interesting, so I peeked out the doorway and into the hall. I was curious about the place and I wanted to see more. The hall was practically empty, except a nurse doing something with a cart on the far end.

As I walked down the hall, I passed some type of waiting room with many chairs, a coffee table, with a television mounted on the wall, tuned to some cable news channel. I briefly looked inside but instead decided to continue my exploration.

I came to an open area with a counter island with several computers and seats in the center of it.

At first, I didn't see anyone but then a nurse behind one of the computer screens popped her head out to the side. "Peter. Wow, I didn't expect to see you up and about so soon," she said. She was a blonde with bright red lips. "Everyone has been talking about you and what you did."

"I didn't do anything special," I said.

"Your friend is in room 309 if you want to see him," she said, pointing to a room a little further down the hallway. "I'm sure he would like to see you."

"My friend?"

"Ralph Higgins," she said, acting surprised that I didn't already know. "The boy you saved."

"Oh, okay. I didn't know he was here," I said, not letting on that I'd rather not visit him.

"I'm sure he'd love to see you," she said, coming around the end of the nurse's station and walking ahead of me to point to his room.

I reluctantly went along, not being able to think fast enough to find an excuse not to see him. If it wasn't for the nurse urging me along, I probably would have gone back to my room. Instead, I inched my way into his room, slowly peering around the corner.

Ralph was sitting upright with the upper half of his bed in an elevated position. He was watching television on the opposite wall when I entered the room. Ralph turned his head and his eyes locked on me, then he turned his head sharply away from me.

I wasn't sure if I should leave or not. My appearance in his room must have caught him off guard and made him feel uncomfortable. I wasn't comfortable either, so his reaction made my decision to leave a whole lot easier. "I'm glad you're okay," I said, turned, and walked to the door.

"Wait!" Ralph called out. "Don't go." He choked back sobs and wiped the tears away with his hands the best he could.

I turned around, not wanting to come back, but not wanting to refuse his request either. I was curious about what he might say to me. The history between us was not pleasant, so my immediate response was to get away from him. However, something was different in Ralph's tone. Something made me stay.

I wheeled my IV tree closer to Ralph's bed, but not too close.

"I'm sorry!" Ralph blurted out among the tears. "I'm so sorry." Ralph began to sob uncontrollably.

It was an uncomfortable feeling to see him cry. A lump swelled up in my throat and I had to fight back the tears.

"Why did you do it?" Ralph asked.

I thought he was mad at me for something – maybe still mad at me for making that goal past him in the hockey game.

"Why did you save me when I have been so mean to you? I don't understand it. I just don't understand it," Ralph wiped the tears from his eyes.

I didn't know how to answer that question. I just know I reacted without really having to think about it. It came from something from inside me and now, faced with having to put an explanation into words, I was finding it difficult.

"I just had to. I don't know. I just did," I said.

Now, since I was able to talk to Ralph when he was being halfway decent, I decided to ask the overwhelming question in my mind, the one that had haunted me day and night. "I always wondered why you hated me so much…I never did anything to you. Why?"

Ralph stayed quiet for what seemed an eternity.

I wasn't sure if he was trying to find the words or he wasn't going to answer.

"It was because of Brenda," he finally answered. "I barely remember her, but I know it tore our family apart. We've never been the same since she died. I've always hated your family for what it did to us."

I didn't know how to respond. "I just found out about the accident," I said after thinking about it. "I didn't even know anything about it until a couple of months ago. I'm sorry for what my father did. I lost a sister too, and I didn't even get to know her at all. My mother and father are struggling with it, too. They have never been the same, either."

Ralph looked surprised. "You mean they never told you?"

"No."

"I guess it was wrong for me to blame you," Ralph said. "I never thought about it that way."

I felt like maybe we both had a lot to think about and the words were not coming easily. I took the opportunity to leave. My head was hurting and I was getting tired. The situation in Ralph's room was emotionally draining. "Well, I hope you get feeling better," I said. "I'll see you later."

"Thank you," Ralph called out, eyes red from crying. "I'm not sure I would have done what you did, but I want you to know that I appreciate you saving my life. I'll never forget it."

"Don't worry about it," I said, a crack of a smile forming on my mouth. I turned to walk out the door, but hesitated in the doorway and turned around. "There's just one more thing," I paused, trying to find the right words. "On the Fourth of July – the fireworks in your house – that was me. I did it. I'm sorry. It was an accident."

Ralph looked surprised. "Oh, that." His mouth abruptly broke into a smile. "That's okay. A real shocker, but not a big deal." His smile grew wider. "I was mad at first, but I got to admit, that was pretty cool."

"Really?" I answered. I broke into a smile too, as I left the room and walked down to my room. I crawled back into my hospital bed.

I felt exhausted, but I fell asleep with a sense of calm—things were going to be all right from now on.

CHAPTER 27
Jeannie Comes for a Visit

~୭

I DON'T KNOW HOW long I was sleeping. The drone of the television provided a good background sound to cover any conversations or noise in the hallway. I don't even know what time it was.

"Knock, knock," someone said, startling me back to consciousness.

My eyes opened to see the Brown family, including Zeke, Jeannie, and their mom and dad, walking through the doorway into my room.

Zeke immediately went up to me at my bedside, looking happy to see me.

Jeannie and her mother and father stood near the end of the bed. Jeannie's eyes were exploring the myriad of plastic lines and the intravenous pump on the stand next to me.

The low grinding sound emanating from the pump and hiss of oxygen reminded me that I was dependent on plastic tubes and a machine for my recovery. I wouldn't be going anywhere until all of it was gone.

"That was cool what you did, man. You saved Ralph's life," Zeke said. "But we were all worried about you when you fell in the water and didn't come up for so long. We thought you were a goner."

"Zeke! Don't talk that way!" his mother scolded.

Zeke's face had a look of surprise as he realized what he had said.

"That's okay," I reassured him, fiddling to straighten out my sheet and blanket.

"Sorry about that. Anyway, you made the news. It was all over television last night. You are a famous dude. Maybe they'll even give you a medal for it." Zeke pumped his fists in unison.

His mother edged forward and put her hand on Zeke's arm. "Now don't get him all riled up," she said sternly. Then she looked sympathetically at me. "We didn't mean to disturb you, Peter. We just wanted to come by and see how you were doing. But Zeke was right. What you did was a very brave thing."

"I don't look at it that way. I just did what needed to be done," I said.

"When are they going to let you out of here?" Zeke asked.

"The doctor said probably tomorrow," I said.

"I just want you to know that we are all praying for you," Zeke's mother said. "When we first heard what had happened, the whole family got together in prayer."

"Thank you," I said, embarrassed to be getting this much attention.

They talked with me a while, all told me they hoped I got better soon so I could return home, and then they walked out of the room.

It was only a minute or so after they left that Jeannie returned to my room alone. She walked slowly up to the side of my bed, a big nervous smile on her face. "Peter," she said softly, laying her hand on mine, "what you did was magnificent. I just want you to know how wonderful I think you are." She looked away for a moment to the window, perhaps to think of what to say next, then returned looking into my eyes. "Maybe ... maybe when you are back at home ... we could do something. You know, maybe go see a movie together or something."

I didn't say anything for a little while, shocked at what she just said. Her hand on mine was nice, something I'd never experienced before. I'd hoped that maybe she might like me. I knew I liked her but never knew for sure what she thought about me. I finally broke into a smile. "Sure. I'd like that," I said, feeling like my face was on fire.

"Okay," Jeannie said, removing her hand. "I'll see you then." She took a few steps backward, then half turned around.

"Oh, just one more thing," I said at the last second before she was gone.

"Yes?"

"Uh." I paused for a moment. "Don't hide in the weeds."

"What?" Jeannie frowned.

"Oh, never mind. It was something Chockie told me to say. I mean ... oh, never mind." I was more embarrassed than ever.

Jeannie chuckled at the humor and my awkwardness. "See ya," she said, turning around and walking out the door.

I let out a big sigh, staring at the ceiling for a moment. "Yes!" I yelled aloud, settling back into my pillow with a big smile on my face.

CHAPTER 28
Father Time

I SLEPT THROUGH THE night with all those tubes running to me, which made my movement a little difficult.

In the morning, the doctor checked on me and cleared me for release, so when my mother came, I was ready and anxious to leave.

The nurse threw together a few items for me, gave me some instructions from the doctor I must follow, such as breathing exercises, and then I changed into the clothes my mother brought me from home. I had to sit in a wheelchair and one of the male nurses wheeled me to the door where my mother picked me up in her car.

"Your father wanted to come along to get you, but he was needed at work this morning," my mother said on the ride home.

"Really?" I asked. I wasn't sure if this was true, or just something my mother said to cover for him.

"Yeah, he really wanted to come. Believe it or not, he was

quite shaken up when we got the news about you. He was crying and very concerned. I think it may have reminded him of the accident that killed Sarah and he probably couldn't deal with losing you, too."

I stopped to think about what she had just said, staring out the car window. "If he cares about me so much, why has he always been angry with me? It's like I can never do anything right. He's always yelling at me for something."

"Honey, he's not mad at you. I know it looks that way and I understand how you think of it that way. The accident tore him up inside and he's been blaming himself ever since. He's been through job after job and became angry with all his friends. He's not mad at you, Peter. He's upset with himself and he doesn't know what he can do to make things right."

As we pulled into the driveway, we noticed my father's Ford F150 pickup truck sitting outside up to the garage door. My mother pushed the remote button attached to the visor and the garage door opened. She drove past my dad's truck and into her side of the garage, where we both got out and grabbed the items from the car to be brought into the house.

The door to the house opened and my dad walked into the garage. "Peter!" he exclaimed, coming over to hug me.

I took it quite stiffly, not embracing him back. I glanced at my mother, puzzled by his greeting and not quite sure what to do.

"I'm glad you're home," my father said. He helped gather the items from the car and walked behind me into the house. The clothes I was wearing while playing hockey were placed into a plastic bag at the hospital, so my mother put them into the washer. I then took my skates downstairs to put them away.

"What are you doing home from work?" I heard my

mother ask my dad. "I thought you had an important meeting."

"I did, but I asked if I could leave early. It was a lot of stuff that didn't pertain to me anyway," he said. "I asked my boss if I could leave and he agreed. I thought to be with my son was more important."

I was surprised by this new interest in me by my father. Until now, I believed my father never had time to show any interest in me or in anything I did.

"It's getting close to lunchtime," my father said. "What would you like, Peter? Would you like a grilled cheese sandwich?"

"Oh my goodness," my mother said. "Don't tell me you're going to cook. I don't remember the last time you ever made anything in the kitchen."

"Yeah, well, there's a first time for everything," he said.

I went to my room, anxious to see Chockie and tell him everything that happened. I dropped some food into the tank, which he snapped up quickly. I wondered if he had been fed while I was away, but I'm sure my mother thought of that. I wanted to talk to Chockie privately, but my mother was hovering nearby, so I waited for a better opportunity.

My father made lunch for everyone and he did so with a sense of happiness I never remembered seeing before. After everyone ate, he insisted on cleaning up and putting everything away.

I went back into my bedroom, firmly shut and locked the door. I sat down on the edge of the bed, happy to see Chockie after all that had happened.

"Hi, Chockie. I'm sorry I haven't been home to take care of you, but they made me stay in the hospital overnight to make sure I was okay." Chockie came to the front of the glass to look at me. "I just can't figure out how you did it. I mean, here you are in the aquarium, yet you were able to get out to help me. How did you get into the pond and back? I just can't figure this out."

I paused for a response.

Chockie remained silent. Wiggling back and forth, he swam up near the surface.

"So, you're still hungry, huh? I bet. Didn't Mom feed you while I was gone?" I dropped some more fish food onto the surface and Chockie quickly snapped them up.

"You won't believe what happened in the hospital. First, Ralph apologized to me. He's not mad at me anymore. I'm pretty sure he's going to leave me alone from now on," I said. "And Jeannie. Jeannie stopped by to see how I was doing. She wants to be friends with me, like go to a movie or something, she said. I can't believe it. Holy cow, Chockie!"

I paused for a response from Chockie. Nothing came, so I resumed, "Dad apologized for being mean to me. He wants to do stuff with me, Chockie! He is like a nice dad now. We are going to do all kinds of things now. We're going to do all those dad-son things, like taking me fishing and stuff."

I stopped suddenly, realizing what I just said. "Fishing. No, Chockie. We won't do that." I shook my head. "I was only kidding. No offense, okay?"

I put my face closer to the tank, looking to see if Chockie was sick or something.

"Why aren't you talking?" I asked. "Look, I'm sorry about the fishing thing if that is what is making you mad. Or are you mad at me because I was gone so long?" I stayed quiet, waiting for a response. "Why won't you say anything?" I grew impatient. "Okay, be that way."

I put on my shoes and headed out my bedroom door. I saw my mother getting out her sewing machine and preparing to work on some clothing projects.

I thought maybe I'd hunt down my dad since now we were going to be good friends. I put on my jacket and stocking cap and went into the garage. I found him under the hood of his car, shining a light with a pistol-like device at the engine while it was running. The overhead garage door was open and a cloud of exhaust smoke trailed into the cold outside air. I stood there for about a minute before speaking, "Can I help?" I asked.

My father looked at me, then back at where he was pointing the flashing light. "Yeah. In a minute, you can shut off the engine for me. Hop in the car and wait until I tell you," he instructed, pointing in the direction of the driver's side front seat. He tightened something on the engine with a wrench, then signaled to me by passing his forefinger across his throat to indicate to shut off the engine.

I turned the key and the engine stopped. I remained in the seat, looking over all the gauges. I didn't remember ever sitting in the driver's seat before.

Checking the air pressure in each of the tires with a gauge, my father came over to my side. "What do you say we take out the Mustang to test it?"

I nodded my head in approval and then slid over to the passenger seat.

My father wiped his hands on a shop towel, got in and backed out of the garage, down the driveway, then turned on the highway away from town.

"You never drive your Mustang in winter. You always say the salt on the road will destroy it," I said.

"That's true. But today is a bright sunny day and the roads are clear and dry. Besides, you only live once." I could see he was deep in thought. "You know, working on this car is a lot of fun for me. It helps me get away from everything else," he said. "I know you have been having problems with

Ralph and I haven't been much help. I just don't know what I can do to help you."

I sat silently for a few moments. "I'll be okay," I said. "Everything is okay now."

My dad drove down a blacktop rural road and went a couple of miles before he pulled over. He opened his door and got out, closing the door behind him.

Walking around the front of the car, he opened the passenger door, much to my surprise. I didn't know what was going on.

"Slide over," he said. I didn't move, not sure I heard correctly. "Slide over to the driver's seat. I want you to take her for a spin."

I moved over behind the steering wheel, a little apprehensive about what would happen next.

My father got into the passenger seat.

"I don't have a driver's license, Dad."

"You can do this. My father let me drive when I was your age and I think it's time I taught you how. I'll help you every inch of the way. It's easy." He pointed at the brake pedal. "Put your right foot on the brake. That pedal there." He pointed to the larger pedal on the left.

I did what he said.

"Now move the selector lever to 'D'," pointing to the gear indicator.

I slid the lever.

"Take your foot off the brake and push lightly on the accelerator pedal, the smaller one on the right. Just push down very slowly."

The car slowly rolled forward.

"You can give it a little more gas," my father said.

The car lurched forward, causing our heads to snap back, but then I was gentler on the pedal and the car began to pick up speed. I felt nervous. Although I knew the basics of what to do and felt confident enough to drive, I was really worried I might damage my father's prize possession.

"You're doing great," he said. "Just go a couple of miles and I'll have you pull over."

After about a mile, I was feeling confident and getting rather bold. I felt like life was good again. Also, I was surprised my dad was allowing me to do this.

Luckily, no other cars were on the road at the time, so I didn't have to worry about the possibility of hitting anybody or anything. When I had driven about two more miles, I pulled to the side of the road where my father instructed and we switched places once more.

When we returned home, I ran into the house to tell my mother. I told her how well I had done – my first time behind the wheel, actually driving a car.

My father soon came in to join in the conversation, "Peter did wonderfully. He's a natural."

I know I had a big smile on my face – I couldn't help it. I started to get a little choked up about it. "Thanks, Dad."

My dad nodded. "When I heard what you did out at the pond and that I might lose you, it woke me up. I realized how much I love you and I wouldn't be able to handle anything bad happening to you. Instead of thinking about what I lost, I should have been thinking about what I have. From now on, I'm going to give an extra effort to be a better person. Please forgive me."

"I forgive you, Dad. I've always forgiven you."

My father pulled me close and hugged me, tears flowing down his cheeks.

I had never seen my father cry before.

That night after supper, I went into my bedroom and told Chockie how my dad let me drive his Mustang. "I found out that my dad is a fun guy. I never knew that until now. He has never really talked to me until now. Yes, sir, things will be much better from now on."

I paused to see if Chockie would answer me.

The gurgling of the aquarium was the only sound in the room.

"Well, if you ever decide to talk again, I'll be here."

CHAPTER 29
A New Beginning

~~~

I KNOCKED ON MRS. Price's door, even though it was already open a foot or so.

Mrs. Price looked over to me from her computer monitor, the soft glow illuminating her face and sending a reflection into her glasses. "Oh, Peter! Come on in. I wasn't expecting you."

I walked over and sat in the same chair as I usually did. "I thought I'd stop in to let you know what happened." I fidgeted with the string on my hooded sweatshirt. It wasn't time for my usual appointment, but I thought I'd let her know I was okay.

"Yes, please do. I was worried about you. When I saw on the news what had happened at the pond, I was praying that you were okay."

"I'm okay. It's something I'll never forget."

"I bet it was," she said, placing her arms on her desk and leaning forward in anticipation. "Tell me about it."

I told the story of how I was playing hockey with the rest of the kids when Ralph fell through the ice and how I helped Ralph out of the water. Then I fell in the water and later woke up in the hospital. I told her how Ralph apologized to me and that my father was spending time with me – like he was a different person. My father smiles a lot and even laughs now, something he never did before. "What was strange is that I saw Chockie there, in the water with me. It was Chockie who helped me through it and got me out of the water."

"So, Chockie was in the pond? How did he get there?" Now she was puzzled.

"That's just it. He was at home when I got there, yet I saw him in the pond."

"Could you have been imagining things? You know, the cold water, the stress of falling in, and the lack of oxygen and everything."

"I have been wondering about that too, but the whole experience was all too real. I could reach out and touch him. He was as real as you sitting here right now. It wasn't a dream or a vision. I know that for sure."

"Well then," she said in an accepting tone. "I'm glad he was there to help you. Have you talked to him about it? Did he explain how he did it?"

I lowered my head and my throat tightened. "No."

"Why not?"

"I don't know. He's just not talking anymore," I said. Talking about it was becoming difficult. I blinked back the tears forming in my eyes.

"Well, maybe he sees that you are okay now and perhaps his guidance is no longer needed," she said with a smile.

I suspected she meant more in her words than what

she'd actually said. "No longer needed? What do you mean? You're saying he only talked because I needed him to talk?" I asked. I couldn't accept this. I sat upright and edged closer to the edge of my chair. "No way. He talks to me because I am his friend." I sat silently, thinking about what she had just said, even becoming a little angry that she suggested such a thing. "You think I made the whole thing up, don't you - that Chockie talks? You never really believed me, did you?"

"I believe you, Peter," she said. "Chockie talking to you is just as real as me talking to you now. It's what you needed in your life." She sighed, taking a moment before speaking again, "Just don't think about it too much. Chockie is your friend and he is still there for you. He will talk again when the time is right. He still loves you just as much as he always has. Just let it go at that."

I blankly stared at the floor, trying to comprehend what she was saying. I glanced up. "I don't know," I said, shaking my head. "I'll just have to give him some time."

"That's right. Be patient. Meanwhile, enjoy your new relationship with your father. I'm sure that has to feel good for you."

My frown changed over to a smile. I laced my fingers together and brought them over my knee. "Yeah. It's really weird now."

"What do you mean, 'weird?'" she asked.

"Well, we're going to a Milwaukee Bucks game this weekend," I said. "I can hardly believe it. He's talking about taking me to a gaming convention in Chicago in April. He is actually thinking about me for a change. He's not even like the same person."

"Maybe he's not the same person," she said, taking me by surprise. "He's a different person, from what you are describing to me and I bet he's just as happy as or happier about it than you. Sometimes bad things happen that turn out to be good things in disguise. He can thank you for that."

I looked into her eyes, trying to piece it all together. "You may be right. I never thought about it that way." The school bell sounded, indicating a change of classes. "I better get going." I rose out of the chair.

"Peter, I am so happy for you. I hope things continue to get better for you. I know you're on the right path. Please come back again sometime and give me an update. Let me know how things are going for you."

"I will." I turned, heading for the door. "Thank you," I said before going out the doorway.

"You're welcome," she said.

CHAPTER 30
Family Hearts Mended

A
FTER SCHOOL, I boarded the bus for the ride home.
The other children were wild as ever, talking loudly
and changing seats. As I walked down the aisle, I
found an open seat about halfway back. As I grasped the
back of the seat and began to turn to sit, my eyes peered to
the back of the bus, catching the sight of Ralph talking with
Shawn and his other buddies.

Ralph looked up and into my eyes just at that moment,
his face cracking a slight smile. His right hand went up and
formed a 'thumbs up' while giving me a slight nod of his
head.

Ralph's friends saw what he had done and then looked
at me.

I responded with a smile of my own and a wave of my
hand before sitting down.

When the bus dropped me off at my house, my heart
leaped when I noticed the garage door stood open and my

mother's car was sitting inside. I felt anxious to tell her how well things had turned around for me at school.

Going through the garage entrance, I walked into the house filled with aromas of a roast in the oven and the voice of my mother singing loudly along with the song on the stereo. She was in the living room, unaware I had entered the house and that I was secretly watching her.

My mother danced a twirl and swung her arms, bobbing up and down.

I could hardly contain himself from bursting out into laughter. I'd never seen my mother dance before.

I stood in the kitchen with my hand over my mouth, holding back laughter. When my mother twisted her feet side to side, shook her hips, bent her knees, and wiggled nearly down to the floor... I lost it. I snorted and then let out a hoot.

My mother abruptly came to a stop and looked over to see me laughing so hard, I was almost doubled over. "Oh, Peter!" she gasped, moving over to me and lowering her head while breaking out into laughter herself. She put her arms around me and pulled me in tightly. "You weren't supposed to see that! I'm so embarrassed."

"Oh, don't worry, Mom. You were doing great. I've never seen you do that before. I've never seen you so happy."

"Yeah, well." She let me go, placing her hands on my shoulders and holding her arms out straight. "I don't know. I just feel good. Things are so much better now." The music was still blaring, so she retreated into the living room to turn down the stereo.

I followed her into the room and abruptly stopped to stare at the walls.

Framed images of Sarah were hanging there – many

pictures. A small hammer and a box of nails lie on the coffee table, evidence of my mother's industrious activities.

Some of the pictures were Sarah's school portraits, some were posed with my mother and father in various locations, yet some were of Sarah doing activities, such as one of her sliding down a waterslide. I spotted one of her in a school play while dressed in some sort of costume, and one of her blowing out candles on her birthday cake.

I was staring at a photo of Sarah sitting in the recliner, the same recliner presently beside me in the living room, with a baby in her lap. I instantly knew the baby was me.

My mother gently put an arm around the middle of my back and pulled me tight to her side. "Yes, that is you," she said. "She cared so much about you. She would play with you and change your diapers. She loved you very much"

Even though I was too young to clearly remember, I could somehow sense the closeness of Sarah back then. My memories of someone with blond hair carrying me and laughing – her face leaning over me and smiling. That had been Sarah… deep inside my memories, I somehow knew.

My mother gave out a huge sigh. "I'm happy to be able to get these out again."

I could see she was cheerful, yet a glint of tears forming in her eyes showed how those were bittersweet memories.

The rumble of a car outside caused us to turn our heads toward the window. I walked over to the big living room window to peer out toward the driveway. I saw a slender young man getting out of his car.

"It's Mitch!" I shouted to my mother.

She didn't say anything but came to the window to look.

I went over to the door and opened it to see Mitch walking up the steps.

"Hey, buddy." Mitch stuck out his hand for a handshake as he stepped inside the house.

I bypassed his hand and wrapped my arms around Mitch in a bear hug.

"I see you still have all your strength," Mitch joked.

I backed away and slapped Mitch on his hand.

"That was quite an ordeal for you, huh?" Mitch asked, then turned slightly to nod to my mother.

"It was no big deal," I said.

"That's not what I heard…Here, this is for you." He handed me a book.

I took it and turned it over in my hands. My mouth dropped open when I saw a color picture of a chocolate cichlid on the cover.

"It's a book of South American tropical fish," he added.

"Oh, man. It's awesome!" I opened the book and looked at the many color photos inside. "I love it. Thank you, Mitch."

"Hey, no problem. I just wanted to come by to see how you are doing. The whole town is buzzing about how you saved that other boy. You are a hero. I hear they're going to erect a statue of you in the park."

"What?" I wasn't sure if I heard correctly.

"Just kidding." Mitch grinned at me. "But you did something amazing, Peter."

"Nah, I'm not a hero. I just did it because someone had to." I was uncomfortable with all the praise. "Mitch, would you want to come and see how big Chockie has grown?"

"Sure," Mitch said and then followed me down the hallway.

When we got into my room, Mitch bent down to have a closer look at Chockie.

"I'm worried, Mitch. Chockie doesn't talk anymore," I said, trying not to seem upset. "I mean, he's eating and he looks the same, but he just won't talk anymore."

"Huh. I don't know what to tell you." Mitch shook his head. "I mean, he looks otherwise healthy, but I've never known any other fish to talk, so I really can't tell you what is going on. Just give it some time – I'm sure he'll come around. It's obvious that you love him and he loves you, so maybe he just needs some time."

"Yeah, I guess so."

Mitch put his hand on my shoulder. "It'll be okay," he assured me.

"Yeah, I'll just give him some time," I said, not sure.

Mitch said he had to get going, so he said farewell to me and Mom.

About 20 minutes after Mitch had left, my father came home. He walked into the living room to stare at all the framed photographs on the walls and those sitting on the lampstand.

My mother and I stood in silence, waiting to see his reaction, not sure if he would be upset or if it brings back the guilt that had plagued him for so many years.

After he scanned all the photos, he finally broke the silence, "Where's the photo of Sarah in the Mustang? That's my favorite one," he said.

We both let out a big gasp and then laughed. The tension was lifted.

"I think it's still in one of the storage tubs," Mom said. "I'll get it."

My dad's eyes twinkled as his mind traveled into each of

the pictures, the outside world with all its trouble gone for the moment.

Later that night, after supper, watching some television, and playing some video games, I got dressed and ready for bed. Exhausted from all that happened during the day, I was anxious to go to sleep. I crawled under the covers and relaxed for a minute, resting my back against the headboard.

For the first time in my life that I could remember, I was at peace with everything in the world.

"Thank you, Chockie, for everything," I said. "You are my best friend. I love you."

I turned out the light, pulled up the covers to my neck, and wiggled my head into the pillow.

Just as I was dozing off, I thought I heard a soft, "I love you too."

Shocked, I sat upright and looked toward the tank. "Did you say something, Chockie? Did you just say 'I love you, too?'"

No answer came.

I laid back down onto my pillow and released a heavy sigh. I did feel sorry that my best friend wouldn't talk to me now, but I always held out hope that he someday.... he would.

Even if Chockie never spoke again, I knew we were the best of friends.

And always would be – forever.